AN
IRISH COUSIN

AN IRISH COUSIN

BY

E. Œ. SOMERVILLE AND MARTIN ROSS

AUTHORS OF

"SOME EXPERIENCES OF AN IRISH R.M.," ETC.

THOMAS NELSON AND SONS, LTD.

LONDON, EDINBURGH, AND NEW YORK

(*Reprinted by permission of Messrs. Longmans, Green and Co.*)

AN IRISH COUSIN.

CHAPTER I.

THERE had been several days of thick, murky weather; dull, uncomplaining days, that bore their burden of fog and rain in monotonous endurance. Six of such I had lived through; a passive existence, parcelled out to me by the uncomprehended clanging of bells, and the, to me, still more incomprehensible clatter which, recurring at regular intervals, told that a hungry multitude were plying their knives and forks in the saloon.

But a change had come at last; and on Saturday morning, instead of heaving ridges of grey water, I saw through the port-hole the broken green glitter of sunlit waves. The S.S. *Alaska's* lurching plunge had subsided into a smooth unimpeded rushing through the water, and for the first time since I had left New York, the desire for food and human companionship awoke in me.

It was early when I came on deck. The sun was still low in the south-east, and was spreading

a long road of rays towards us, up which the big
steamer was hurrying, dividing the radiancy into
shining lines, that writhed backwards from her
bows till they were lost in the foaming turmoil
astern.

A light north wind was blowing from a low-lying
coast on our left, bringing some faint suggestions of
fields and woods.   I walked across the snowy deck, to
where a sailor was engaged in a sailor's seemingly
invariable occupation of coiling a rope in a neat
circle.

" I suppose that is Ireland ? " I said, pointing to
the land.

" Yes, miss ; that's the county Cork right enough.
We'll be into Queenstown in a matter of three
hours now."

" Three hours more ! " I said to myself, while I
watched the headlands slowly changing their shapes
as we steamed past.   This new phase of life that
had once seemed impossible was now inevitable.   My
future was no longer in my own control, and its secret
was, perhaps, hidden among those blue Irish hills,
which were waiting for me to come and prove what
they had in store for me.

" First breakfast just ready, miss," said one of the
innumerable ship-stewards, scurrying past me with
cups of tea on a tray.

I paid no attention to the suggestion, and made my
way to a deck chair just eagerly vacated by a hungry
old gentleman.   I could not bring myself to go
below.   The fresh kind wind, the seagulls glancing

against the blue sky, the sunshine that gleamed broadly from the water and made a dazzling mimic sun of each knob and point of brasswork about the ship,—to exchange these for the fumes of bacon and eggs, and the undesired conversation of a fellow-passenger, seemed out of the question.

The sight of the land had given new life to expectations and hopes from which most of the glory had departed during the ignominious misery of the last six days. I lay in my deck chair, watching the black river of smoke that streamed back from the funnels, and for the first time found a certain dubious enjoyment in the motion of the vessel, as she progressed with that slight roll in her gait which the sea confers upon its *habitués*.

Most people appear to think that sea-sickness, if spoken of at all, should be treated as an involuntarily comic episode, to be dealt with in a facetious manner. But for me it has only two aspects—the pathetic and the revolting; the former being the point of view from which I regard my own sufferings, and the latter having reference to those of others. In the dark hours spent in my state-room, I had had abundant opportunity to formulate and verify this theory, and I have never since then seen any reason to depart from it.

CHAPTER II.

To Miss Sarsfield, S.S. "Alaska," Queenstown.
From W. Sarsfield.

" Awfully sorry I will not be able to meet you.
Drive to Foley's Hotel.   Will be waiting you there."

This despatch was put into my hand before I left
the steamer at Queenstown.   Its genial tone and eccentric grammar were quite in keeping with my ideas
of an Irishman.   These were at once simple and
definite.   All Irishmen were genial ; most of them
were eccentric.   In fact, had my uncle and cousin
met me on the pier, clad in knee-breeches and tail-
coats, and hailed me with what I believed to be the
national salutation, " Begorra ! " I should scarcely
have been taken aback.

The outside car on which I drove from the Cork
station to the hotel was also a realisation of precon-
ceived ideas.   In response to the bewildering proffers
of " Inside or outside ? " I had selected an " outside,"
and was quite satisfied with the genuineness of the
difficulty I found in remaining on it, as we rattled
through the muddy streets.   The carman himself was
perhaps disappointing.   His replies to my questions

were not only devoid of that rapartee which I had understood to be the attribute of all Irish carmen, but were lacking in common intelligence; and on his replying for the third time, " Faith, I dunno, miss," I concluded I must have hit on an unlucky exception.

The day had lost none of the brilliancy of the early morning. It seemed to me that the sun shone with a deliberate intention of welcome, and the unfamiliar softness of Irish air was almost intoxicating. Everything was conspiring to put me into the highest spirits; I laughed when my new dressing-bag was flung on to the pavement by the dislocating jerk with which the car pulled up in front of Foley's Hotel.

As I walked into the hotel, the porter who had taken in my boxes went over to a tall young man who was leaning over the bar at the end of the narrow hall, and whispered something to him. He immediately started from his lounging position, and, furtively glancing at the mirror behind the bar, he came up to me.

" How do you do? I'm very glad to see you over here," he said, with an evident effort to assume an easy cousinly manner. " I hope you didn't mind not meeting me. I was awfully sorry I couldn't get down to Queenstown, but I had important business in town." It was perhaps a consciousness of the interested scrutiny of the young lady behind the bar that caused him to blush an ingenuous red as he spoke. " You'd better come on and have some luncheon," he continued, without giving me time to answer him. " We've only got an hour before the train starts."

I followed him into the coffee-room, thinking as I did so how different this well-dressed, rather awkward young man was from the picturesque and vivacious creature I had somehow pictured my Irish cousin to be. His accent, however, was unmistakably that of his native country ; or, rather, as I afterwards found, that of his particular part of it. His quick, low way of speaking was at first rather unintelligible to me, and almost gave me the idea that what he said was intended to be of a confidential nature ; but on the whole I thought his voice a singularly pleasant one.

By the time our luncheon was put on the table he was more at his ease, and had even, with a sheepish half-deprecating glance from his light grey eyes, addressed me as " Theo." The fraternal familiarity of the head waiter was, on Willy's explanation that I was his cousin from Canada, extended in the fullest degree to me.

" Indeed, when I seen her coming in the door, I remarked to Miss Foley how greatly the young lady favoured the Sarsfield family," he observed blandly ; " and Miss Foley said she considered she had a great likeness to yourself, captain."

This was a little embarrassing. I did not quite know what I was expected to say, and devoted myself to my mutton-chop.

" I did not know that you were a soldier," I said, as soon as the waiter had gone.

" Oh, well," replied my cousin, giving a conscious

twist to his yellow moustache, " I'm only a sort of one
—what they call ' a malicious man.' I'm a captain
in the West Cork Artillery Militia," he explained ;
" but nobody calls me that but the buckeens here-
abouts."

I wondered silently what a buckeen was, and why
it should be so anxious to maintain the prestige of the
militia, but did not like to betray too much ignorance
of what might be one of the interesting old courtesy
titles peculiar to Ireland.

Looking at my cousin as he rapidly devoured his
luncheon, I noticed that, in spite of his disclaimer of
military rank, he took some pains to cultivate a
martial appearance. His straw-coloured hair was
clipped with merciless precision, and on his sunburnt
forehead, a triangle of white, obviously cherished,
marked the limit of protection afforded by an
artillery forage-cap.

" I think I'd better be looking after your luggage
now," he said, bolting what remained of his second
chop, and getting up from the table, with his mouth
full. " I was quite frightened whan I saw those two
big mountains of trunks coming along on the car
after you. And then when I saw *you* walk in "—he
laughed a pleasant, foolish laugh—" I didn't think
you'd be such a swell ! " he ended, with confiding
friendliness.

The terminus of the Cork and Esker railway, the
line by which we were to travel to Durrus, was
crowded on that Saturday afternoon. We had ten
minutes to spare, during which I sat at the window

and watched with the utmost interest the concourse on the platform. It had all the appearance of a large social gathering or conversazione. Stragglers wandered from group to group, showing an equal acquaintance with all, and displaying entire indifference as to the intentions of the train, while the guard himself bustled about among them with an interest that was evidently quite unofficial. My carriage soon became thronged with people, between whom and their friends on the platform a constant traffic in brown-paper parcels was carried on ; and I was beginning to think there would be no room for Willy, who had disappeared in the crowd. But the ringing of the final bell set my mind at rest, as I found that, contrary to the usual usage, this sound had the agreeable effect of almost emptying the train.

Willy returned at the last moment, emerging from the centre of a group of young ladies, with the well-pleased air of one whose conversation has been appreciated.

" Did you see those girls I was talking to ? " he said as we moved out of the station. " They're cousins of the O'Neills, people in our part of the world. They came down to see me off. There was a great mob there to-day, but there always is on a Saturday."

" The O'Neills are neighbours of ours," Willy continued. " They live at Clashmore—that's four miles from us—and they're very nice people. Nugent, the brother, used to be a great pal of mine—at least, he was till he went to Cambridge, and came back thinking no one fit to speak to but himself."

Not feeling particularly interested in the O'Neills, I did not pursue the subject; but Willy was full of conversation.

" I'm just after buying a grand little mare in Cork. It was that kept me from going to meet you," he observed confidentially. " I suppose you learnt to ride at your ranch, Theo? I tell you what: I bought her for the governor to drive, but she'd carry you flying, and you shall hunt her this winter if you like."

My cousinly feeling for Willy increased perceptibly at this suggestion.

" But," I said, " if your father buys her, he will want to ride her himself, won't he? "

" Is it the governor? "—with an intonation of contempt. " You never see *him* on a horse's back. He's always humbugging in the house over papers and books. I believe he used to be a great sportsman and fond of society, but he never goes anywhere now."

The two ladies who had started from Cork with us had got out a station or two afterwards, and we had the carriage to ourselves. But the extraordinary jolting and rattling of the train were not conducive to conversation, and, seeing that I was not inclined to talk, Willy relapsed into the collar of his overcoat and the Cork newspaper, and ended by going unaffectedly to sleep.

It grew slowly darker. I sat watching the endless procession of small fields slipping past the window,

until the grey monotony of colour made me dizzy.
I leaned back, and, closing my eyes, tried to imagine
the life I was going to, and to contrast its probabilities
with my past experience. But a strange feeling of
remoteness and unreality came upon me. I suppose
that the mental exhaustion caused by so many new
sights and impressions had dazed me, and I began to
doubt that such a person as Theo Sarsfield had ever
really existed. Willy, my Uncle Dominick, and my
father flitted confusedly through my mind as inconsequently as people in a dream. I myself seemed to
have lost touch with the world ; my past life had slid
away from me, and the future I had not yet grasped.
I was a solitary and aimless unit in the dark whirl
that surrounded me, and the sleeping figure at the
opposite end of the carriage was a trick of imagination
and as unreal as I. I became more and more remote
from things actual, and finally fell from all consciousness into a sleep as sound as Willy's.

My slumbers were at length penetrated by a shriek
from the engine. I sat up, and saw that Willy was
taking down his parcels from the rack ; and in another minute we were in the little station of Esker.

A hat with a cockade appeared at the window.

"Hullo, Mick. Is it the dog-cart they've sent ?"

"'Tis the shut carriage, Masther Willy," said Mick ;
"and 'tis waiting without in the street."

With some difficulty I followed Mick through the
crowd of carts in the station yard, to where a landau
and pair were standing in the road. The moonlight
was bright enough for me to see the fine shapes of

the big brown horses, who were evincing so lively an interest in the caprices of the engine that the coachman had plenty to do to keep them quiet.

"You're welcome, miss," said that functionary, touching his hat; and I got into the carriage, followed by Willy, with the usual impedimenta of male travelling youth.

"It's a good long drive," he said, arranging rugs over our knees—"twelve Irish miles. But we don't be very long getting there. You won't have time to be tired of me—I hope not, anyhow."

This was more like my idea of the typical Irishman, but was, nevertheless, rather discomposing from a comparative stranger. It was said, moreover, with a certain conquering air, which plainly showed that Willy was not accustomed to being found a bore. I could think of no effective reply, so I laughed vaguely, and said I hoped I should not.

We had been driving at a good pace for about an hour, when we left the high road and began the ascent of a long steep hill. At its summit the carriage turned a sharp corner, and I saw below me, on my right, a great sheet of water all alight with the misty splendour of a full moon. Black points of land cut their way into the expanse of mellow silver, and the small islands were scattered like blots upon it.

"That's Roaring Water Bay," said Willy; "and that mountain over there's called Croagh Keenan "— pointing to a shadowy mass that formed the western limit of the bay. "You haven't anything to beat that in Canada, I'll bet!" An assertion which I refrained from combating.

Our road now lay for a mile or two along the top of a hill overlooking the bay, and though Willy had spared no efforts to beguile the way for me, I was tired enough to be extremely glad when the carriage swung sharply between high gate-posts, and we entered the avenue of Durrus.

As we passed the lodge, I caught, in the moonlight, a glimpse of the pretty face of a girl who opened the gates, and asked who she was.

"She's the lodgekeeper's daughter," said my cousin.

"She looked very pretty."

"Yes, she's not bad looking," he said indifferently. "There are plenty of good-looking girls in these parts."

The drive sloped down through a park to the level of a turf bog, which it skirted for some distance, and then entered a thick clump of trees, through which the moonlight only penetrated sufficiently to let me see that they were growing in a species of reedy swamp, from which, on this cold night, a low frosty mist was rising. We were soon out again into the moonlight, the horses quickening up as they came near their journey's end. I saw a sudden gleam of sea in front, and on the left a long, low house, looking wan and ghostly in the moonlight.

CHAPTER III.

As the carriage drew up at the hall door it was opened by a stout elderly man, who came forward with such empressement that for a moment I thought it was my uncle. Providentially, however, before I had time to commit myself, he exclaimed :—

" Your honour's welcome, Miss Sarsfield ! "

Willy checked further remark on his part by shovelling our many parcels into his arms ; but as soon as we had got into the hall, he let them all go, and caught hold of my hand and kissed it.

" Glory be to God that I should have lived to see this day ! I never thought I'd be bringing Masther Owen's child into this house. Thank God ! thank God ! "——He hastily let go my hand, as a tall bowed figure came across the hall to meet me.

" Well, my dear Theodora, so you have found your way at last to these western wilds," said my Uncle Dominick, and kissed me on the forehead, taking both my hands in his as he did so.

His manner was an extreme contrast to Willy's affable familiarity, and I was struck by the absence of Irish accent in his voice, which was of a mellifluous not to say alarming propriety.

He led me into the room he had just left, a small library, and placed a chair for me in front of the fireplace.

"You must be cold after your long journey. Sit down and warm yourself," he said politely, adding another log to the furnace that was blazing in the brass-mounted grate.

He rubbed his long white hands together and drew back, so as to let the light of the lamp fall on my face.

"And your uncle and aunt in Canada—Mr. and Mrs. Farquharson—you left them quite well, I hope? I daresay they resent your desertion very bitterly?"

I explained that the two years of ranch life that I had spent in Canada since my mother's death had not appealed to me, and that, in a household of twelve, the blank caused by my departure could not be irreparable. "In fact, I am thankful to get back to Great Britain again!" I concluded, warming one frozen foot after another, while my uncle stood with his back to the lamp, and surveyed me with guarded intentness. From his letters I had expected him to be formal, in an old-world, courteous way, but this strained and glacial geniality was a very different thing, and it disconcerted me considerably.

It was a distinct relief when, at this juncture, Willy came in, and offered to show me the way to my room. We passed through the dark entrance-hall, whose depths were inadequately lighted by a cheap lamp, its orange light forming a dingy halo that contended hopelessly with the surrounding gloom. At the end of the hall was a broad flight of stairs, that at the first

landing branched into two narrower flights leading to
a corridor running round the hall. Passing along one
side of this corridor, Willy opened a door at the end
of it.

"Here you are," he said; "and I told them to
bring you a cup of tea; I thought you looked
as if you wanted it"—with which he took his departure.

I was touched by Willy's unexpected hostess-like
thoughtfulness in the matter of the tea. My uncle's
reception had chilled me. I was tired by my long
journey, and the darkness and silence of the house had
a depressing effect upon my spirits. For weeks this
arrival at my father's old home had been constantly
in my mind, staged and acted by myself with a vast
outlay of enthusiasm and hope; now that it was over
the enthusiasm had gone as dead as flat champagne,
the hope was drowned in disillusionment, even in
foreboding.

I looked round me as I sipped my tea, and did not
feel enlivened by what I saw. The room was large
and bare. The paper and the curtains of the two
windows were alike detestable in colour and pattern.
The enormous bed had once been a four-poster, but
the posts had been cut down, and four meaningless
stumps bore witness to the mutilation it had under-
gone. A colossal wardrobe loomed in a far-off corner;
a round table of preposterous size occupied the centre
of the room. Six persons could comfortably have
dined at the dressing-table. In fact, the whole room
appeared to have been fitted up for the reception of

a giantess, and was quite out of proportion to my
moderate stature of five feet seven.

I have always disliked more than one door in a
bedroom, as it seems to me to afford to ghosts and
burglars unnecessary facilities; and my dislike of my
gaunt apartment reached its climax when I saw a
door in the corner on the farther side of the fireplace
from the door into the corridor.   It had been papered
over along with the walls, and was almost suspiciously
unobtrusive.   I opened it, and found that it led into a
moderate-sized bedroom. The moonlight which came
through the uncurtained window lay in greenish-white
patches on the uncarpeted floor, and showed a few
pieces of furniture, shrouded in sheets and huddled in
one corner.   In spite of its chill bareness, an effect
of recent occupancy was given to it by a chair that
stood sideways in the window, a few tattered books
on the floor beside it.

I went back to my own room with an unexplainable
distaste, slamming the door behind me, and proceeded
to dress for dinner with all speed.

With the unfailing punctuality of a newcomer, I
left my room as the gong sounded, and, hurrying
down, found my uncle and Willy waiting for me in
the library.

The dining-room was a large and imposing room.
A moderate number of portraits of the most orthodox
ancestral type hung, interspersed with mezzotints of
impassioned Irish clergymen, on its panelled walls.
A high old sideboard of what seemed to me an unusual shape stretched up to the ceiling on one side of

the room, and the plate upon it twinkled in the blaze of the fire.

We sat down at the long table; and while Willy and his father were absorbed in overcoming the usual embarrassments offered by soup to the wearers of moustaches, I amused myself with speculations as to who was responsible for the subtle combination of yellow and magenta dahlias that adorned the table. I concluded that the artist must have been the old butler, Roche; and as, at the thought, I involuntarily looked towards him, I found his eyes fixed upon me with the abstracted gaze of one who is trying to trace a likeness. Our eyes met, and he shuffled away, but I felt sure that he had been searching for a resemblance to the irregular attractive face which, from a miniature of thirty years ago, I knew must be what he remembered of my father. I sincerely hoped he found it.

"It is quite an unusual pleasure to Willy and me to see a charming young lady at our bachelor-table—eh, Willy?" said Uncle Dominick, lifting his face from his now empty soup-plate, and smiling at me.

Willy, whose flow of language seemed checked by his father's presence, gave an assenting grunt.

"It is a long time since there has been a Miss Sarsfield at Durrus, and it is thirty years since she died. You will find Willy and I are sad barbarians, and we shall have to trust to you to civilise us."

I am quite unfitted to deal with the compliments of elderly gentlemen. On this occasion I failed as signally as usual to attain the requisite quality of playful confusion. and diverted the conversation by a question about a claret-coloured ancestor, who had been staring at me from his frame over the fireplace ever since we had sat down to dinner.

"That is my grandfather," said my uncle. "Dick the Drinker, they called him. He neither is nor was an ornament to the family ; but his wife, the beautiful Kate Coppinger, is worth looking at. In fact, my dear "—with another smile and a little bow— "directly I saw you I was reminded of a miniature which we have of her."

"I hope she looks Irish," I responded. "I have always tried to live up to my idea of an Irish girl ; but though my hair is dark, I haven't got violet eyes."

"No, nor any one else either. I never heard of them out of a book," said Willy, abruptly.

It was almost his first contribution to the conversation ; but his father took no more notice of him than if he had not spoken, and went on eating his dinner, taking longer over each mouthful than any one I had ever seen.

"Then, am I not like the Sarsfields ? " I asked.

My uncle paused and looked hard at me for a second or two, letting his heavy eyebrows drop over his eyes, with a peculiar change of expression.

"In some ways, perhaps," he said shortly. Then, turning to Willy, " Nugent O'Neill was here this afternoon to see you about the stopping of some earths. I told him to come over and dine here some day next week. Not "—turning to me—" that he is much of a ladies' man, but he is a gentlemanlike young fellow enough ; very unlike his father," he added, in a bitter tone.

" Why, is Mr. O'Neill very objectionable ? " I said.

I felt an unmistakable kick under the table, and Willy, with an admonitory wink, slurred over my question by saying :—

" I can tell you, O'Neill would be pretty mad if he heard you calling him *Mr*. He's *The* O'Neill, and his wife's Madam O'Neill, and they wouldn't call the queen their cousin."

My uncle silently continued his dinner, but I noticed how unpleasant his expression had become since The O'Neill was mentioned.

I finally made up my mind that his face was one I should never care for. He was decidedly a handsome man, though unusually old-looking for his age, which could not have been more than sixty.

His thick dark eyebrows lay like a bar across his high forehead. A long hooked nose dropped over an iron-grey moustache, which, when he smiled, lifted in a peculiar way, and showed long and slightly prominent yellow teeth. His unwholesomely pallid skin was deeply lined, and hung in folds under the dark sunken eyes, giving a look of age which was further contributed to by the stoop in his square shoulders. As I glanced from him to Willy, I concluded that the latter's blonde commonplace good looks must have been inherited from his mother.

Rousing himself from the morose silence into which he had fallen, my uncle proceeded to apply himself to the task of entertaining me by a dissertation on the trade and agriculture of Canada. I soon found that he had all the desire to impart information which characterises those whose knowledge of a subject is taken from pamphlets ; but I listened with all politeness to his description of the country in which I had spent the past two years. Willy maintained a discreet silence, but from time to time bestowed on me glances of sympathy and approbation. Evidently Willy did not know how to talk to his father.

As dinner progressed, I observed that, if Roche allowed his master's glass to remain empty, he was at once given a sign to refill it, and my uncle became more and more diffusely instructive.

During dessert a pause at length gave me an opportunity of changing the conversation.

" I saw such a pretty girl at your gate lodge as we drove in," I said. " She looked delightful in the moonlight, with a shawl thrown over her head."

If Uncle Dominick had looked black at the mention of The O'Neill, he became doubly so at this apparently inoffensive remark. Glancing for explanation to Willy, I was amazed to see that he had become crimson, and was elaborately trying to show his want of interest in the subject by balancing a fork on the edge of his wine-glass.

" Yes," said my uncle ; " she is a good-looking girl enough, and no one knows it better than she does. When people in that class of life are taken out of their proper place "—with great severity—" they at once begin to presume."

Willy upset his wine-glass with a sudden jerk. For

my part, I was so taken aback by this tirade, that
I thought my safest plan lay in immediate flight.
Willy got up with alacrity, and, following me from
the room, opened the drawing-room door. He
looked confused and annoyed.

"Can you take care of yourself in there for a
while?" he said. "I'll be with you in a few
minutes."

CHAPTER IV.

THE room was cold ; I at once made for the fire, and, to my surprise, found the hearthrug occupied by an untidy little girl, who was engaged in dropping greese from a candle over the coals to make them burn. On seeing me she sprang to her feet, and, with apologetic murmurs, she gathered up a coal-box and retired in confusion.

I concluded that, improbable as it appeared, this was the under-housemaid, and reflected with some astonishment on the incongruities of the Durrus establishment. However, I afterwards found she held no official position, but was a satellite of the under-housemaid's, privately imported by her as a species of body-servant or slave. In fact, at the risk of digressing, I may here add that in process of time I discovered that the illicit apprenticeship of a young relation was a common custom of the Durrus servants, and in the labyrinthine remoteness of the servants' quarters they could be concealed without fear of attracting the master's eye.

In spite of its top dressing of grease, the fire was not a tempting one to sit over, and I roamed round the large ill-lighted room, taking in with amazement the varied style of its decorations. It was, in startling contrast to the rest of the house, painted and papered in semi-æsthetic hues, pale sage green and pink being the prevailing colours. This innovation of culture had not, however, extended itself to the furniture, which was of the solidly ugly type prevalent fifty years ago. Heavy mahogany tables, each duly set forth with books and daguerreotypes, stood uncompromisingly about, causing a congestion among the lesser furniture. The pictures, which had been taken down at the repapering of the room, leaned against the wall with their faces inwards. I turned one of the nearest to me, expecting to come upon a family portrait, but found it represented a Turk of truculent aspect, worked in Berlin wool—a testimony to the amount of spare time at the disposal of the ladies of Durrus. The thick coating of dust on my fingers which was the result of this investigation did not encourage me to make any further researches, and an examination of the old china on the marble chiffonnier between the windows had equally disastrous results. In one corner there was an ancient grand piano, which to my astonishment proved to be in good tune. I had not been playing for very long when Willy came in, and, without speaking, placed himself beside me.

" Well, I declare ! " he said, as I finished playing one of Schubert's impromptus, " it's a long time since I heard that old piano. I got it tuned the other day on purpose for you, and you know how to knock sparks out of it, anyhow ! I heard Henrietta O'Neill playing that piece once, and it didn't sound half so well—though, I can tell you, she thinks no end of herself."

" By-the-bye, Willy, why did you stop me when I began to speak of Mr. O'Neill ? "

" O'Neill," corrected Willy.

" Oh, well, *O'Neill*, but what was the harm of talking about him ? "

" No harm, as far as I am concerned, but the governor hates him like poison. I believe they had some row in my grandfather's time—I don't know exactly what—and they never made it up since. But there's no regular quarrel ; I go to all their parties, and I think the governor rather likes Nugent and the girls."

" What is Madam O'Neill like ? "

" Oh, *I* get along with her first-rate," said Willy, stretching out one of his long legs, and serenely studying the gold-embroidered clock on his sock. " But other people say she's rather a bitter old pill ; and I can tell you, she has the two girls in great order ! "

I began to play as he finished speaking ; but his thoughts had travelled on to my other unlucky remark at dinner, for he presently interrupted me by saying in an uncertain way :—

" Oh ! you know that girl we were talking of at dinner, the one you saw at the gate—Anstice Brian her name is—her mother is a bit queer in her head, and she'd be very apt to give you a start if you didn't know her ways. She's a harmless poor creature, but she wanders about these bright nights, and she gets into the house sometimes."

I probably looked as alarmed as I felt, for he laughed protectingly, and, drawing his chair a little closer to mine, said reassuringly :—

" Never fear ! She's not half as silly as they say ; and do you think I'd let her be about if there was any chance at all of her frightening you ? "

" What is she like ? Is she an old woman ? "—ignoring the reproachful warmth of this last observation.

" Is it old Moll Hourihane ? She's as old as two men—or she looks it, anyhow. She used to be my nurse till she went off her head."

" I thought you said her name was Brian," I said.

" That's only her husband's name. The women mostly stick to their own names in this country when they're married."

" And you're quite sure she's not dangerous ? " I said, feeling only half reassured.

" No more than I am myself "—with a glance to see if I were going to contradict this assertion. " She has a sort of dumb madness—like a hound, you know —and she'll never speak ; though I dare say after all that's no great loss," he concluded.

I was by this time feeling very sleepy, and hoping I should soon be able to escape to my own room, when the door opened, and my uncle came solemnly in.

" I have come, Theodora, my dear, to suggest an early retirement on your part."

He avoided looking at Willy, and I felt that the

effects of my ill-timed remarks at dinner had not yet died out. He looked haggard and troubled, and a sudden pity and sense of kinship impelled me to raise my cheek towards him as he took my hand to say good-night. He stooped his head as if to kiss me, but checked himself, and after an instant of hesitation his moustache touched my forehead. He turned and left the room, and I heard him go back to the library and shut himself in, the sound of the closing door emphasising his solitariness.

I went upstairs with the feeling of isolation again strongly upon me. The wind had risen, and on the walls of the draughty corridor each gust made the old pictures shake in their shabby frames. At intervals, through the panes of the large skylight overhead, the moon's light dropped in pale wavering squares on the floor on the hall below. I leaned over the balustrades, watching the spectral alternations of light and darkness, as the clouds swept across the moon, till the objects beneath me seemed to take intermitting motion from the flitting of the moonbeams.

As I looked, the dim lamp in the hall flickered and went out. A gust from below circled round the corridor, lifting the hair upon my forehead and almost extinguishing my candle as it passed me.

Perhaps I was overtired and nervous, but the old childish dread of some vague pursuit out of the darkness clutched me. I gave a terrified glance over my shoulder at the swaying pictures, then, shielding my candle with my hand, I ignominiously ran down the corridor into my own room.

CHAPTER V.

" WILL you have your tay, plase, miss ? "

The words at first mingled with the dreams which had all night disturbed my sleep. On being repeated, the unfamiliar accent, accompanied by the clink of a cup and saucer, made me open my eyes. A pleasant-looking, red-haired girl was standing by my bed, tray in hand.

" You're after having a great sleep, miss. I was twice here before, and there wasn't a stir out of you."

" Is it very late ? " I asked, with an alarming recollection of my uncle's punctuality.

" Oh, not at all, miss. The masther's only just after having his breakfast."

" What ! " I gasped. " You should have called me earlier."

" Oh, there's no hurry, miss ! Sure he always ates his breakfast by himself, and there's no sayin' how late it'll be before Masther Willy's down."

Calmed by this assurance, I did not hurry myself over my dressing, but from time to time stopped to look at the view from my windows.

It was a quiet October day, with a grey yet luminous sky, that lit with a grave radiance the group of yellow elms that divided the avenue from a heathery expanse of turf bog, with low hills beyond. From the other window, which was almost over the hall door, I could see to the left a dark belt of trees that stretched to the back of the house ; and in front, at the foot of the lawn, the curve of a little bay. This was separated from the larger waters of Durrusmore Harbour by a low promontory, along whose ridge a meagre line of fir-trees was etched against the grey sky. Leaning out of the window, and looking westwards towards the mouth of the harbour, I saw the Atlantic lying broad and white under the light of the soft clear morning.

I went downstairs, and as I passed along the corridor, I felt, even on this still day, the draught from broken panes in the skylight and the staircase window, making it easy to account for the ghostly eddyings of the wind the night before.

Willy had apparently made an effort on my behalf at early rising, and I found him making tea when I came into the dining-room. He came forward to meet me with a complacency in which I detected a consciousness of the added smartness of his Sunday attire ; and, having ascertained the fact that I had slept well, he installed me behind the urn to pour out the superfluously strong tea which he had just brewed.

There was immense relief in the absence of Uncle Dominick, whom at this moment I saw pacing up and down a walk leading from the house to the sea. Willy followed the direction of my eyes.

" I hope you're not insulted by only me breakfasting with you," he said, with ungrammatical gallantry. "You can breakfast with the governor whenever you like, but you will have to be down at eight o'clock to do that!"

I intimated with fitting politeness that I was satisfied with the present arrangement, and we began our *tête-à-tête* meal in great amity. Willy, indeed, was an excellent host. He plied me with everything on the table, eating his own breakfast and talking all the time with unaffected zest and vigour, and I began to feel as if the time I had known him could be reckoned in months instead of hours.

The necessity of writing to announce my safe arrival to Aunt Margaret was one that had already forced itself upon my notice.

"I thought you'd be wanting to write a letter," Willy said, conducting me into the drawing-room after breakfast, "and I got the place ready for you." I sat down at the old-fashioned writing-table, and found that he had anticipated my wants with a lavish hand. Through the window I saw him, a few minutes afterwards, sauntering down the drive towards the lodge, smoking a cigarette, with two little white fox terriers flashing in circles round him; and as I watched him, I came to the conclusion that at first sight I had under-estimated my cousin.

There was something to me half amusing and half touching in the anxiety of his little housewifely attentions to me. He was really unusually thoughtful for others; from various things he had said, it was evident that his father had allowed the whole manage-

2

ment of the place to devolve on him, and I fell to idle speculation as to whether he ordered dinner, and if he were particular about the housemaids wearing white muslin caps; and I was only aroused from these, and other equally interesting reflections, by hearing the clock strike the hour at which I had been warned I must get ready for church.

My uncle was standing on the steps, with his Prayer-book in his hand, when I came downstairs. He wished me good-morning, with a polite apology for not having met me at breakfast, and stood looking about him, with eyelids narrowed by the white glare from the sea, till a minute afterwards the waggonette in which we were going to church came to the door. My uncle and I got in behind; while Willy, with Mick by his side, sat on the box and drove. Once outside the gate, we took a road running at right angles to that by which I had arrived. It went round the head of Durrusmore Harbour, and, leaving the sea behind, turned inland through large woods, which my uncle told me were part of the demesne of Clashmore, The O'Neill's place.

The road was level, and soft with the fallen red beech leaves, and the brown horses took us along it at a pace that showed they were none the worse for their journey the night before. The rough stone walls on either side of the road were covered with moss and small ferns. Here and there the wood was pierced by narrow rides—vistas in which the clumps of withering bracken repeated the brown and gold of the trees above.

"We're going to draw this place on Friday," said Willy, pausing in the steady flow of his conversation with Mick to give me the information. "Blackthorn will carry Miss Theo right enough, wouldn't he, Mick? and I'll ride the new mare."

The village of Rathbarry, which we had now entered, consisted of a single street of low, dirty-looking cottages, their squalid uniformity varied at frequent intervals by the more prosperous shuttered face of a public-house. At the end of the street, a gateway led into a graveyard, surrounded by ill-thriven elm-trees, in the middle of which stood the church. It was an ugly, oblong building, with a square tower at the west end, from which proceeded a clanging as of a cracked basin battered with a spoon.

"We're in good time," said Willy, drawing up with a flourish before the porch. "That's the hurry-bell only begun now, so we've five minutes to spare. Look. Theo! there's the Clashmore carriage. Did you ever see such brutes as those chestnuts?"

Before, however, I had time to reply, Uncle Dominick hurried me into the church, and we took our places in opposite corners of a singularly uncomfortable square pew. As we sat confronting each other in the half-empty church, we heard in the porch Willy's voice raised in agreeable converse. Apparently his remarks were of a complimentary sort, for a girl's voice rejoined, "Oh, nonsense, Willy!" with a laugh.

"Disgraceful!" muttered my uncle, under his breath; and the next moment three ladies swept up the aisle, followed by Willy, on whose face still beamed a slightly fatuous smile.

He immediately sat down beside me, and in a rapid whisper instructed me as to the more prominent members of the congregation.

" Those are the O'Neills "—indicating the ladies he had come in with. " Connie's the little fair one. And look ! those are the Jackson-Crolys ! You'd better sit up and behave, as they'll be watching you all the time. I know they all want to see what you're like ! "

" Hush ! don't talk ! " I whispered back. " Here's the clergyman."

The service was very long. The music, which consisted of the clergyman's daughter accompanying herself on a harmonium, with casual vocal assistance from a couple of school-children, was of an unexhilarating kind. Willy fidgeted, admired his boots, trimmed his nails, and tried to utilise every possible opening for conversation. Uncle Dominick, on the contrary, devoted his whole attention to the service, and answered all the responses with austere punctiliousness, even going so far as to try and track the clergyman's daughter in her devious course through the hymns.

From the corner which had been allotted to me in my uncle's pew I could not see the clergyman, and, though his voice resounded through the church, his very pronounced Cork accent made it difficult for me to understand more than a word here and there in his discourse.

The high sides of the pew debarred me from even

the solace of inspecting the congregation, and, in the absence of other occupation, I could not altogether conceal the interest that I felt in the remark which Willy was laboriously spelling on his fingers for my edification. Becoming conscious, however, that Uncle Dominick's eye, while fixed upon the preacher, had included us in its observations, I transferred my attention to the mural tablets, which on either side of the church set forth the perfections of dead-and-gone O'Neills and Sarsfields.

Having studied these for a few minutes with the mild sceptical interest usually excited by the tabulated virtues of the unknown departed, I leaned back in my corner, and, in doing so, noticed a brass upon the wall slightly behind my uncle's seat. My eye was immediately caught by my father's name.

IN MEMORIAM

THEODORE WILLIAM SARSFIELD,

WHO DEPARTED THIS LIFE

JANUARY 10, 185–.

AND OF

OWEN SARSFIELD,

SON OF THE ABOVE,

WHO DIED SUDDENLY IN CORK,

ON HIS RETURN FROM CANADA,

JANUARY 9, 186–.

THIS MONUMENT IS ERECTED BY THEIR SORROWING SON AND BROTHER, DOMINICK SARSFIELD, OF DURRUS.

I glanced by a natural transition to my uncle, whose head all but intervened between me and the brass. His expression of sombre melancholy harmonised well with the words " his sorrowing brother."

I could guess what must have been his grief at the death of an only brother. Till then I had scarcely realised how closely linked their lives must once have been, and I resolved that his chilly manner should not deter me from some day inducing him to speak to me of my father.

As I made up my mind to this, the clergyman's voice ceased, and the congregation rose at the end of the sermon. We walked out of church close behind the O'Neills, and outside the porch Madam O'Neill stopped to shake hands with my uncle. Then, turning to me :—

" I need not ask to be introduced to you, my dear. I knew your poor father very well indeed in days gone by." This was said in a dry, attenuated voice, but through the elaborate pattern of her Maltese lace veil, her eyes looked kindly at me. She was small and refined looking, with little artificial airs and graces which told that she had been a beauty in her day ; and what remained of a delicate complexion was carefully sheltered from the harmless light of the grey sky by a thick parasol.

Uncle Dominick's impatience to get away only gave me time to say a word or two in answer to her salutation.

" Come, Theodora," he said, with the smile that

lifted his moustache and showed all his teeth. "We must not keep the horses waiting."

Willy was already on the box of the waggonette, and was talking to a dark, quiet-looking young man who was standing with one foot on the wheel.

"Then you'll see about having those earths stopped," Willy said, leaning over, and emphasising what he was saying with the handle of the whip on his hearer's shoulder. "Oh, here they are! Theo, let me introduce Mr. O'Neill. I was just telling him he must be sure and have a fox for you at Clashmore this week."

"I'll do my best," said Mr. O'Neill, as he took off his hat; but he did not look particularly enthusiastic as he spoke.

We had no sooner driven off, than Willy twisted round on the box to speak to me.

"Well, what do you think of Nugent?" he said rather eagerly.

"He is nice-looking," I replied critically; "but he looks as if he thought a good deal of himself."

"Oh, he's not half a bad chap," said Willy, with a leniency which was possibly the result of the pleasure with which young men listen to the depreciation of their fellows. "He's decent enough sometimes; but he can put on a bit of side when he likes, and I dare say he thinks he is thrown away down here. Henrietta's like him in that sort of way, but Connie has no nonsense about her."

I decided that Connie's was the laugh that I had heard in the porch before service, and thought that of the two I should be more likely to prefer Henrietta.

Ever since we had left church the sky had been darkening, and when we reached Durrusmore Harbour, the distant headlands were almost hidden in a white mist. The south-west wind blew it towards us from the sea, and by the time we got home a thick fine rain was coming steadily down.

Lunch, with Uncle Dominick at the head of the table, was a more serious business than breakfast had been, and old Roche's shuffling ministrations added to the general solemnity. I was, however, amused by the affectionate solicitude with which he nudged me in the elbow with the dish of potatoes, indicating with his thumb a specially floury one, and concluded that this was his singular method of showing respect for my father's memory.

When lunch was over Willy announced his intention of walking to Clashmore, to see about borrowing a side-saddle for me, he said—an act of self-sacrifice which I was not slow to attribute to the fascinations of Miss Connie O'Neill. Uncle Dominick retired to a private den at the end of a dark passage leading from the hall to the back of the house ; and a few minutes later Willy, in a voluminous mackintosh, set forth on his errand, followed by the fox terriers in a state of amiable frenzy, the result of the abhorred Sunday morning incarceration. I became aware that I was thrown upon my own resources, and, with the prospect of a wet afternoon before me, I felt my spirits sinking perceptibly.

To finish my letter to Aunt Margaret was at least better than doing nothing. I took up a strong position in front of the library fire, and disconsolately applied myself to filling the big sheet of foreign paper on which I had embarked in the morning.

CHAPTER VI.

WILLY did not come home till dinner-time, when he reappeared in exceedingly good-humour. I, on the contrary, felt the vague ill-temper of a person who has spent a wet Sunday afternoon in solitude, and I found dinner long and dull. In the drawing-room, after dinner, I sought the resource of music to raise my spirits ; but I was debarred from even this last consolation, for Willy implored me to " let the piano alone," as his father disapproved of music on Sunday.

We finally settled down in arm-chairs, and I discovered that Willy possessed in a high degree the feminine faculty of sitting over a fire and talking about nothing in particular. He pretended to no superiority to the minor gossip which forms the ripples in the current of country life, and he had quite a special gift of recounting small facts with accuracy and detail, and without any endeavour to exalt his talent as a story-teller. His tales had, in consequence, a surprising freshness and merit, and till bedtime we maintained a desultory, but on the whole enjoyable conversation.

When I got up to my room, I found it full of smoke and extremely cold. The window had been opened to let out the smoke, and the chintz curtains rustled and flapped in the draught. Making up my mind after a few minutes that even turf smoke was preferable to the cold disquiet of the wind, I went to the window to close it, and discovered that, the pulley being broken, the housemaid had supported the sash with one of my brushes.

There was something in this misplaced ingenuity which was eminently characteristic of the slipshod manner of life at Durrus, and by force of contrast my thoughts travelled back to my mother's orderly household. I leaned against the shutter and looked out, beset by poignant recollections of a time when life without my mother seemed an impossibility, and when Durrus was no more to me than a place in a fairy story.

The wind had blown away most of the fog, and the rain had ceased, but a thin haze still blunted the keenness of the moonlight. I gazed at the dark shapes of the trees in the shrubbery till I lost the sense of their reality, and they came and went like dreams in the uncertain light. In my ears was still the throb and tremor which seven days and nights spent in listening to the screw of the *Alaska* had imprinted on my brain, and my thoughts and surroundings seemed alike hurrying on in time to that inveterate pulsation. I was at length aroused to realities by a sound which at first seemed part of the light chafing of the laurel leaves, but which in a few moments became detached and distinct from the vague noises of the autumn night.

It came nearer, and gave the impression of some stealthy advance in the wet grass under the trees. At length, at the verge of their shadow, just opposite my window, I heard the gravel crunch under a soft footstep. A woman's figure slid into the dim light, and came out across the broad gravel sweep with a swaying gait, as though moving to music.

Half-way to the house she stopped, and, raising her arms above her head with a wild gesture, she began to step to and fro with jaunty liftings and bendings of her body, as though she were taking part in a dance. Backwards and forwards she paced with measured precision ; then, placing her hands on her hips, she danced with incongruous lightness and vigour some steps of a jig. Suddenly she checked herself ; she knelt down, and, turning a pale face to the sky, she crossed her hands on her breast and remained motionless.

Her absolute stillness was almost more dreadful than the strange movements she had previously gone through, and I stood staring in terror at the grey kneeling figure, with the rigid face turned skywards in what appeared to be the extremity of supplication. Just then the moon shone sharply out, hardening and fixing in a moment the limits of light and darkness, and, as if with a sudden movement, it flung the shadow of the praying woman on the ground before her. She started, and slowly rose to her feet, and, with her hands still crossed on her bosom, turned her face towards me. I saw the moonlight glisten in her wide-open eyes, which were fixed, not on me, but on the window of the room next to mine. Then, opening her arms wide, she let them fall to her side with an elaborate curtsy and sidled back into the impenetrable shadow of the trees.

I stood bewilderedly staring at the spot where the darkness had swallowed up her figure; before I had time to collect my ideas, she reappeared at a little distance, and, as well as I could see, turned up a path which led through the shrubbery in the direction of the lodge.

As she passed out of sight, I remembered in a flash what Willy had said to me about Anstey's half-witted mother. It was a simple explanation, and perhaps a humiliating one; but, in spite of my anxiety to possess a ghost-story of my own, I accepted it with relief. I shut the window and locked my door, and, though still trembling all over with cold and fright, I went to bed, thankful that "Mad Moll" had introduced herself to me from without, instead of first appearing to me within the walls of Durrus.

CHAPTER VII.

" And so she gave you a great fright ? Well, now, wasn't that too bad ? I wish I'd caught her at her tricks, and I'd soon have packed her about her business. You know, they say she was the best step-dancer in the country when she was a girl ; and to think of her going dancing under your window, and you taking her for a ghost ! "

Willy's amusement overcame his sympathy, and he laughed loud and long.

I had been impelled to confide my alarm of Sunday night to him when we were on our way round to the stables to see the horses, on the following morning, and I now rather resented his refusal to see anything but the absurdity of the incident.

" You are very unsympathetic. I am sure you would have been just as frightened as I was," I said. " She looked exactly like a ghost ; and in any case I should like to know why she selected *my* window to dance under ? "

" She meant it for a compliment, of course. I suppose she thought you'd be a good audience. *I've* seen her now and again jack-acting there in front of the house, but I'm afraid all I said was to tell her go home. But then, I'm not sympathetic like you ! "

We had stopped to discuss the point at the spot whence I had seen Moll emerge, and now walked on past the untidy old flower-garden to the yard.

It was a large square, of which three sides were formed by stables and cowhouses, the house itself being the fourth, and was only redeemed from absolute ugliness by a row of four great horse-chestnut trees, which grew out of a grassy mound in the middle. We arrived in time to surprise the two little fox terriers, Pat and Jinny, in the clandestine enjoyment of a meal with the pig, whose trough was conveniently placed by the scullery door. On seeing us, they at once endeavoured to dissemble their guilty confusion by an unworthy attack on their late entertainer. This histrionic display did not, however, deceive Willy in the least. The dogs were ignominiously called off, and the pig was left master of the situation.

I wondered, as I looked round, if all Irish yards were like this one. Certainly I had never before seen anything like the mixture of prosperity and dilapidation in these solid stone buildings, with their rickety doors and broken windows. Through the open coachhouse door I saw an unusual amount of carriages, foremost among them the landau in which I had driven from Esker, with a bucket placed on its coachbox in order to catch a drip from the roof. A donkey and a couple of calves were roaming placidly about, and, though there was evidently no lack of stable-helpers and hangers-on, everything was inconceivably dirty and untidy.

The horses were, however, well housed and cared for. My future mount, " Blackthorn," was the first to be displayed. He was a strong black horse, with a roach back and an ugly head, but he had a wise face and a kind and quiet eye. In the next box, the bay mare Willy had bought in Cork was pushing her nose through the bars over the door to attract our attention.

" That's the one kept me from going to meet you at Queenstown," said Willy, opening the door, and catching the mare by the head. " She's a smart little thing, but I'll know better another time than to throw you over for her. Stand, will ye ! " as the mare made a vigorous remonstrance at being deprived of her sheet.

" She looks as if she knows how to go," I said. " What are you going to call her ? "

" Don't you think you might christen her for me ? " Willy answered, with an insinuating glance at me from under his black eyelashes. " Just to show you don't bear malice for my leaving you to cross Cork all alone."

Notwithstanding the access of brogue with which this was said, there was something in the look which accompanied it at which, to my extreme annoyance, I felt my colour rise.

" Of course I don't bear malice. I never even expected you to meet me," I said, turning to stroke the mare's shoulder. " If you really want a name for her, suppose you call her ' Alaska.' That was the steamer I came over in, and they say she's the fastest on the line."

Willy received this moderate suggestion with enthusiasm. " If she turns out half as good as she looks," he said, as we walked out of the yard, " you shall have her for yourself to ride."

" I think you are very rash to put me up on your horses when you don't in the least know how I can ride."

" Ah ! well, I'll trust you ! Though, indeed, after the funk you were put into by poor old Moll, I suppose I may expect to see you turning back at the first fence."

To this sally I vouchsafed no reply.

" I must take the mare out this afternoon," he continued, " to try can she jump. Blackthorn wants shoeing, or you should ride him ; but I thought perhaps you'd like to walk up to the farm to see me schooling the mare. It's only as far as those fields opposite the lodge that I'll go."

This was, I thought, a very good suggestion. A prospective day with the hounds made me extremely anxious to see what Irish fences were like, and my experiences at my uncle's ranch in Canada had not included double banks and stone walls.

At lunch Uncle Dominick was more conversational than I had yet seen him.

" What have you been doing with yourself this morning, Theo, my dear ? "—for the first time adopting the more familiar form of my name.

" The roses in your cheeks do credit to our Irish
air."

Uncle Dominick's faded gallantry always had the
effect of making me feel like a fool, and before I could
rise to the occasion Willy struck in :—

" She was round to the stables with me, sir."

" Oho ! so that was it, was it ? " said my uncle,
with the smile I disliked so much ; and I felt that
at that moment my cheeks more resembled peonies
than roses.

" I was showing her the new mare," said Willy,
" and we're going to call her ' Alaska,' because that's
the ship that "—here he stopped—" because that's
the fastest ship between this and America."

" Why, is not that the vessel that brought you
to us from America ? " said Uncle Dominick, pursuing his advantage with unexpected facetiousness.
" I think it is an admirable name, and will always
have pleasant associations for you and me, eh,
Willy ? "

Willy made no reply, and my uncle rose from the
table, apparently well satisfied with himself, and left
the room humming a tune.

It was a softly brilliant afternoon. I thought, as I
started for the farm where I was to see Alaska put
through her paces, that I had never, even in Canada,
seen anything like the glow of the yellow leaves
against the blue sky—a blue so intense that it seemed
to press through the half-stripped branches. The
thick drifts of fallen leaves rustled like water about
my feet, and floated on the surface of the pools which

the rain of yesterday had formed in the low swampy ground under the clump of elms at the bend of the avenue. Just here a deep dyke ran parallel with the drive, separating it from the great tract of turf-bog that I had seen from my bedroom window. At right angles from it another similar weedy water-way stretched starkly across it to the distant silver of a small lake. Where the two joined there was a rough pier of large stones, and a dilapidated flat-bottomed boat, used for bringing turf for the house, was tied to an alder tree. Across the dyke was a bridge of logs, from which a raised cart track wound over the bog like a long brown serpent. I crossed the bridge and leaned upon the rusty iron gate that closed the approach to the bog road ; the keen scent of the sea came to me across the heathery expanse, mingled with the pure perfume of the peat, and I regretted that my promise to Willy prevented me from following the devious course of the cart track over the headland to where I heard the hollow draw of the sea on the rocks at the other side.

Retracing my steps, I went up the avenue, and found Willy, seated on Alaska, and accompanied by the two dogs, waiting for me outside the entrance gates. In the fence on the other side of the road was an opening partially filled by a low wall of loose stones—locally called a gap.

"I'll take her in at this gap," Willy said, turning the mare to give her room, and then putting her at the gap. Alaska, however, had probably her own reasons for preferring the road, for she refused with an adroit swerve, and a lively contest between her and her rider ensued.

The latter's difficulties were considerably complicated by Pat and Jinny, who, with ostentatious activity, insisted on crossing and recrossing the gap at the most critical moments. When Jinny at length took up a commanding position on its topmost stone, in order to watch, with palpitating interest and ejaculatory yelps, Alaska's misbehaviour, it seemed time for me to intervene, and snatching her from what she doubtless felt to be the front seat in the dress circle, I held her wriggling in my arms, until at length Alaska, with a bound that would have cleared a five-barred gate, went into the field.

I climbed on to a gate-post, from whence I could conveniently see the schooling process. Neither my school days at Stuttgart, nor various sojournings in Swiss pensions with my mother, not even my two years of ranch life in Canada, had equipped me as a critic of the performance, but it was not difficult to see that Willy was master of the situation, and that Alaska had realised the fact in all its bearings. It was interesting to watch, but it was also rather cold, and after a chilly quarter of an hour spent on my gate-post, I left Willy in search of further educational difficulties and decided to go home without him.

Outside the Durrus entrance gates was a large gravel sweep, with high flanking walls, forming a semicircular approach, and in these, at some height from the ground, several niches had been made, large enough to hold life-sized figures. As I climbed down from my gate-post I saw that a young girl was standing in one of the niches. She was leaning slightly forward, steadying herself with one hand on the wall, while with the other she shaded her eyes, as if looking after Willy's departing figure.

On seeing me, she jumped quickly down, and ran to open one of the small gates. I recognised the shy, charming face of Anstey Brian, and stopped inside the gate to speak to her.

" If Mr. Sarsfield comes, will you tell him I have gone home ? " I said ; and was turning away, when Anstey, with a nervous blush, said, in a soft, deprecating voice—

" Oh, miss, I beg your pardon ! I was very sorry to hear you got anny sort of a fright from my mother last night. It's just a little restless she is, those last few nights, and my father'd be greatly vexed if he thought you got anny annoyance by her."

I told her I had not really been frightened, while I wondered a little how she had heard anything about it.

" Indeed, miss, she'd hurt no one. She's this way, foolish-like, this long time."

" How long is it since it began ? " I asked, while I wished my hair would curl as attractively as hers.

" I never remember her anny other way, miss, though my father says she was once a fine, handsome girl, and as sensible as yourself, miss."

" Did her mind go from an accident ? " I asked.

" Why, then, indeed, miss, I don't rightly know

She had some strange turn in her always, and afther I was born she got quare altogether ; and that's the way she is ever since. Dumb, like she couldn't spake, and silly in her mind."

I was looking in the direction of the lodge while she spoke, half unconsciously noting how thickly the ivy trails hung over its small windows, when I became aware of a face looking out at me through one of them.

I could distinguish little of it beyond the wide-open, pale eyes, which were fixed upon me with concentrated, half-terrified intentness ; but with a momentary return of last night's panic, I knew it to be the face of the woman of whom we were speaking. Something of this must have been shown in my expression, for Anstey, following the direction of my eyes, said—

" Don't be frightened at all, miss. Will I bring her out here for your honour to see ? "

But I had no wish for any close acquaintance, so hastily saying that, as it was already dark, I had no time to stay, I wished Anstey good-night.

I must confess that, as I walked away from the lodge, I was haunted by the frightened stare of Moll Hourihane's eyes. There had been something in their expression which, beneath the oblivion of insanity, seemed almost to struggle into recognition. At the remembrance of them, I felt the same pursuing dread creep over me again, and I hurried along the avenue towards home. To my imagination, the patches of grey lichen on the trees repeated in the growing twilight the effect of the grey face at the darkened window. The dead leaves awoke as I trod on them, and followed me with whisperings and cracklings. It was a relief to leave the little wood behind, and to see in the library windows the flickering glow which told of a good fire, and suggested tea.

I was surprised and annoyed by the nervousness which had lately come upon me. I prided myself upon being a singularly practical, unimaginative person ; and yet now, for the third time since my arrival at Durrus, my self-possession had been disturbed by a trivial event, which I should formerly have laughed at. I walked rapidly to the house, determined for the future to give no toleration to my foolish fancy, and to——

"Here you are !" said Willy's voice from the hall door. "Come on and have some tea."

CHAPTER VIII.

It occurred to me several times during the next few days how strangely little I saw of my uncle. Except at luncheon and dinner, he seldom or never appeared, even in the evenings preferring to sit alone over his wine in the gloomy dining-room, while Willy and I were in the drawing-room. At ten o'clock regularly the door would open, and his tall austere figure would appear, holding my candle ready lighted ; and with the same little speech about the advantages of early hours for young people, he would wish me good-night, politely standing at the foot of the stairs as I went up. As a rule, I did not see him again until luncheon next day, and I wondered more and more how he spent his time.

Willy seemed to know little more about his father's occupations than I did.

" Oh, *I* don't know what he's up to," he had said, when I asked him. " He prowls about the place from goodness knows what awful hour in the morning till breakfast, and he sits in that den of his all day, more or less. I've plenty to do besides watching him."

Whether or not this was Willy's real reason for

avoiding his father, it was a sufficiently plausible one.
All outdoor affairs at Durrus were under his control,
and at any time during the morning he might be seen
tramping in and out of the stable, or standing about
the yard, giving orders and talking to the numerous
workmen in a brogue in no way inferior to their own.

I may mention here that Willy, in common with
many Irish gentlemen when speaking to the lower
orders, paid them the delicate, if unintentional, compliment of temporarily adopting their accent and
phraseology. I had plenty of opportunities of noti-
cing this, as Willy evidently considered that the
simplest method of providing for my amusement
was to take me about with him as much as possible.
I had at first rather dreaded the prospect of these
constant *tête-à-têtes*, but I soon found that my cousin
had always plenty to talk about, and was one of the
few men I have met who were good listeners.

He contrived to include me in most of his comings
and goings about the place. He took me down to
the cove to see the seaweed carried up the rocks on
donkeys' backs to be spread on the land ; or I
watched with deep interest while the great turf-
house was slowly packed for the winter with the rough
brown sods ; or, standing at a little distance, I listened with respect to his arbitration of a dispute
between two of the tenants, who generally accepted
his verdict as if it had been a pronouncement of the
Delphic oracle. He was very popular with the country people, as much perhaps from his invincible
shrewdness as from his ready good-nature, and sub-

sequent observation has shown me that nothing so much compels the respect and admiration of the Irish peasant as the rare astuteness that can outwit him.

Thursday was fair day at Esker, and Willy, who regarded the attending of fairs as both a duty and privilege, proceeded thither with the first light of day. To say at cock-crow would scarcely be an exaggeration, for, knowing well the absurdity of expecting any servant within the walls of Durrus to call him, he had—so he informed me—resorted to the device of putting over-night a vigorous barn-door cock on the top of his wardrobe. The cock's conscientious announcement of dawn was, as may be imagined, of a sufficiently rousing character, and in consequence Willy's arrival at even the most distant fairs was as a rule timely.

The result of his absence was a solitary morning for me, and lunch alone with Uncle Dominick. Although faintly alarmed at the latter prospect, I was at the same time glad of the chance which it offered. I had not yet abandoned the romantic hope of winning the heart of my father's only brother.

But, regarded as a first step in this direction, luncheon was a disappointment. My uncle did not abate an atom of his usual impenetrable civility, and conversed with me on entirely uninteresting topics, with a fluency that was as admirable as it was provoking. I was absolutely at a loss to understand him, and puzzled myself a great deal as to what he thought about me. The compliments which he never lost an opportunity of making, and his evident desire that

Willy should do all in his power to make my visit agreeable to me, were not, I felt sure, any real indications of his feelings. That he took an interest in me, I was certain. Often I surprised in his cold eyes a still scrutiny, a watchful appraising glance that suggested mistrust, if not dislike; and although his manner was distant and self-engrossed, I had a conviction that little that I said or did escaped him.

It was a depressing day. A quiet rain trickled steadily down, and through the blurred windows the trees looked naked and disconsolate against the threatening sky. I made up my mind that it was not a day to go out, and, with a pitying thought of Willy at the fair, I heaped turf and logs upon the library fire, and determined to fall back upon the last refuge of the destitute, and to write a foreign letter.

After a period of virtuous endeavour with this intent, I discovered that I was becoming bored to stupefaction, and gave up the struggle. There was something in the air of Durrus antagonistic to letter-writing; or perhaps it was the impossibility of writing about a place which was so different from anything that I or my correspondents had been accustomed to, and was at the same time so devoid of interest for them. I bethought me of a certain old book of field-sports which Willy had commended to my notice, and I wandered round the dusty shelves, looking for it among the exceptionally uninteresting collection of books which formed my uncle's library. Not being able to find it, I took the bold step of going to his room to ask him if he could tell me where it was.

As I went down the long dark passage that led to his room, I was keenly alive to the temerity of the proceeding, and knocked at the door with some trepidation.

"What is it?" came an unencouraging voice from within.

"Oh! I only wanted to ask you about a book, Uncle Dominick," I began.

The door was opened almost immediately.

"Come in, my dear Theo," said my uncle, with what was intended for a smile of welcome. "What book is it you want?"

I explained, adding that Willy had recommended the book to me.

"Oh, Willy told you of it, did he?" said my uncle, with interest; "and you cannot find it in the library?"—turning towards a large cupboard that filled a recess on one side of the chimney-piece. 'Perhaps I have it in here."

I heard a faint jingle of glass as he opened it; but the doors of fluted green silk, latticed with brass wire, prevented, from where I was standing, my seeing inside. My uncle ran his finger along one of the shelves in search of the book I wanted. Meantime I looked curiously about me.

It was a small, dingy room, disproportionately high for its size, with county and estate maps hanging on its damp-stained walls. A handsome old escritoire stood in the corner to the right of the lofty window that faced the door by which I had entered. On one or two tables, dusty pamphlets and papers

lay about in a comfortless way. Right in front of
the fire was a battered leather-covered arm-chair, in
which my uncle had been sitting, though there was
no book or newspaper to indicate that he had been
occupied in any way.

"It is an unusual thing to hear of Willy recom-
mending a book. I suppose this is due to your
civilising influence?" said my uncle, emerging from
the recesses of the cupboard with the book in question in his hand.

"Oh, well," I replied, laughing, "this is not a very
high class of literature."

"It is, nevertheless, a classic in its way," he said,
opening the book; "and the prints are very good
indeed."

I came and stood beside him, looking at the illus-
trations with him.

"The Regulator on Hertford Bridge Flat," "The
Race, Epsom," "The Whissendine Brook"—we
studied them together, Uncle Dominick becoming
unexpectedly interesting and friendly in his reminiscences of his own sporting days when he was a
young man at Oxford.

As he paused in looking at the pictures to enlarge
upon an experience of his own, the pages slipped
from his stiff bony fingers, and, turning over of their
own accord, remained open at the title-page. There
I saw, in faded ink, the words, "Owen Sarsfield, the
gift of his affectionate Brother, D. S."

My uncle looked at the inscription for half an instant, and, drawing a quick breath, closed the book.

"Uncle Dominick," I said, with a sudden impulse, "won't you tell me something about my father? My mother could never bear to speak of him, and I know so little about him."

He turned his back to me, and replaced the book in the cupboard, feeling for its place in the shelves in a dull, mechanical way.

"I hate to give you pain," I went on; "but if you knew how much I have thought about him since I have been here! I have always so connected him and Durrus together in my mind."

He walked back to the fireplace, and placed one hand on the narrow marble shelf before answering.

"There are many circumstances connected with your father which make it painful for me to speak of him," he began, in a quiet, measured voice. "I loved him very dearly; we were always together until his lamentable quarrel with my father."

He walked to the window, and stood looking out through the streaming panes, with his hands behind his back. After a few moments of waiting for him to speak again, I could bear the silence no longer.

"But what was the quarrel about? Was it my father's fault?"

"It is a hard thing to say to you," replied my uncle, turning round and looking past me into the fire, "but, under the circumstances, I feel that it is my duty to let you know the truth. Your father unfortunately got into money difficulties while at Oxford, which he was afraid to mention to my father. He went to London to study for the Bar with these debts still hanging over him, while I came home and undertook the management of the property." He paused, and passed a large silk handkerchief over his face. " Owen always had a passion for the stage ; he got entangled with a theatrical set in London, and finally he took the fatal step of making himself responsible for the expenses of an—in fact, of a travelling company of actors, with, I need hardly tell you, what result. Instead of the enterprise paying his debts, as he had hoped, he found himself liable for large sums of money."

Uncle Dominick came back to the fireplace, where I was standing nervously grasping the shabby back of the leather arm-chair. I suppose my face told of the anxious conjectures that filled my mind, for, looking at me not unkindly, my uncle went on :—

" I did all I could for him with my father, but he was a man of very violent temper, and was absolutely infuriated with Owen. He paid the debts, but he refused to see Owen again, and insisted on his leaving the country. I contrived to see him before he left England, and a few years afterwards he wrote to tell me of his marriage with your mother, but from that day until I heard of his death in Cork, I neither heard of nor from him."

" But," I broke in, " why did he never write to you ? "

My uncle hesitated, and drew his hand heavily over his moustache. I saw that it trembled. He sat down in the chair by which I stood, and did not answer. I put my hand on his shoulder.

"Surely he had not quarrelled with you, Uncle Dominick? Or was it that you—that you thought he had behaved too——" I could not finish the sentence.

"No, no, my dear," he said quickly; "I had no such feelings. I would have done anything in the world for him at that time." He cleared his throat and continued huskily: "It was Owen who misjudged me, who misconstrued all my efforts on his behalf, who ignored my offers of assistance. I cannot bear to think of what I went through," he ended hastily, leaving his chair and again walking to the window. It was a French window, and a few stone steps led from it to the grass outside. He opened one door and looked down the drive.

It was getting darker, and the rain came driving in from the sea in ghost-like white clouds; he stood there motionless, and apparently oblivious of the drops that fell from the roof on his head and shoulders.

"Are you looking out for Willy?" I said at length.

"Oh, Willy! Yes; is he not home yet?" he answered absently, closing the window.

"Is there any portrait of my father in the house?" I asked, as he turned towards me, ignoring his remark about Willy in my anxiety to put a question that since my arrival at Durrus I had often wished to ask, and feeling that it might not be easy to find another opportunity of reopening the subject.

"There is one, taken when he was a child; it hangs in the corridor outside your bedroom door."

" But I think there are two portraits of boys there," I persisted. " I am afraid I should not know which was his."

My uncle rose wearily from his seat. " If you wish, I will show it to you now," he said. " If you will go upstairs, I will follow you in an instant."

I went slowly up the passage, and before I had reached the foot of the stairs he overtook me, and we went up together. He had his crimson silk handkerchief in his hand, and I remember wondering why he kept pressing it to his mouth as we walked along the corridor side by side.

A faint light shone through the open door of the room over the hall door, the one that opened into mine, and against the grey light I saw in the window a crouching figure indistinctly silhouetted.

My uncle saw it too. With a muttered exclamation of anger, he walked quickly past me to the open doorway.

" What are you doing here ? " he said sternly. " You know I desired you not to come upstairs, and this is the second time this week I have found you here."

He stepped back to one side, and a tall woman with a shawl covering her bent shoulders shuffled out of the room. I had already guessed that it was Moll Hourihane, and I shrank back into the doorway of my own room ; but she stopped, and, stretching out her neck towards me, she fixed her eyes upon my face with an expression of hungry eagerness.

" Did you hear what I ordered you ? Go down at

once," repeated my uncle, placing himself between her and me. " Let me never find you here again."

She immediately turned and slunk away round the far side of the corridor, and, looking back once more at me, disappeared through the door that led to the servants' quarters.

I gave a sigh of relief. " That woman terrifies me," I said. " I wish she would not look at me in that dreadful way."

" You need not be alarmed "—he spoke breathlessly and with unusual excitement—" she is perfectly harmless ; but I do not choose to have her roaming about the house. These are the pictures of which we were speaking," he continued. " The one to the right was done of me, and this—this is the other " —pointing to an old-fashioned-looking portrait of a pretty dark-haired boy holding a spaniel in his arms.

CHAPTER IX.

" On the first day of March
In the year '43
The first recreation
In this counthry,
The King's County gentlemen
O'er hills, dales, and rocks,
They rode out so gallantly in search of a fox !'

WILLY'S voice was light-hearted enough to match my
own feelings, as Blackthorn, looking sedately amiable,
was led up to the hall door next morning. In spite
of a fast-beating heart I felt as I looked at him that
I might safely trust him to initiate me into the mysteries of cross-country riding in the county Cork.

The day was lovely—sunny and mild, with a lingering dampness in the air that told of light rain during
the night. I settled myself in the saddle, intoxicated
by the idea that I was actually going out hunting for
the first time, though I could not help a tremor of
anxiety as I wondered if Willy would find his confidence in me had been misplaced.

I could hear him now in the hall, knocking down
umbrellas and sticks in search of his whip, and
presently, in response to his shouts, old Roche came
shuffling to his aid.

"I was putting up your sandwiches, sir," he said.
"Go on, and give hers to Miss Theo, and hurry,"
said Willy's voice, in a tone indicative of exasperation.

Roche bustled out on to the steps with a small
packet in his hand, a jovial smile on his face. He
looked at me, and his face changed.

"My God! 'tis Master Owen himself!" he said,
as if involuntarily. "I beg your pardon, miss," he
continued, coming down the steps and putting the
sandwiches into the case. "I suppose 'twas the
man's hat, and the sight of you up on the horse,
made me think of 'Heir Sarsfield,' as we called your
father."

Willy, at all times a carefully attired person, was
to-day absolutely resplendent in his red coat and
buckskins, and as we rode slowly down the avenue,
I was impelled to tell him how beautiful both he
and the mare looked. He beamed upon me with a
simple satisfaction.

"Do you think so? Well, now, do you know what
I was thinking? That no matter how good-looking
a girl is, she always looks fifty per cent. better on a
horse!"

"That is a most ingenious way of praising your
own horse," I said.

"Ah now, you know what I mean quite well," rejoined Willy, with a look which was intended to be
sentimental, but, by reason of his irrepressibly good
spirits, rather fell away into a grin.

The meet was to be at the Clashmore cross-roads,
and we passed many people on their way there.

White-flannel-coated country boys and young men
—" going for the best places to head the fox," as
Willy explained, and chattering swarms of National-
School children. Every now and then a young farmer
or two came clattering along, on rough, short-necked
horses, whose heavy tails swung from side to side as
they trotted at full speed past us, and an occasional
red coat gave a reality to the fact that I was going out
fox-hunting. The cross-roads were now in sight, and
I saw a number of riders and people who had driven
to see the meet, waiting for the hounds to come up.

"Why, I declare, here are the two Miss Burkes
coming along in that old shandrydan of theirs with
the bedridden grey pony!" said Willy, looking back.
"Hold on, Theo. I must introduce you to them;
they're great specimens."

We allowed the pony-carriage to overtake us, and
Willy, pulling off his hat with as fine a flourish as his
gold hat-guard would allow, asked leave to introduce me.

"With the greatest of pleasure, Willy. Indeed,
we'd no idea till yesterday, when we met Doctor
Kelly in town, that Miss Sorsefield had arrived."
This from the elder Miss Burke, a large, gaunt lady
with a good-humoured red face and an enormous
Roman nose, and a curiously deep voice, whose
varying inflections ran up and down the vocal scale
in booming cadences.

"You ought to be riding the pony, Miss Burke.
She looks in great form."

"Oh, now, Willy! you're always joking me about

poor old Zoé. You're very naughty about him. Isn't he, Bessy ? "

The younger Miss Burke, thus appealed to, replied with a genteel simper, " Reely, Mimi, I am quite ashamed of the way you and the captain go on. Don't ask *me* to interfere with your nonsense ! We hope, Miss Sarsfield "—turning a face that was a pale dull replica of her sister's towards me—" to have the pleasure of calling upon you very soon. But oh, my gracious ! there are the dogs and Mr. Dennehy coming ! And look at us keeping you delaying here ! Good-bye, Miss Sarsfield. I hope you'll obtain the brush ! "

At the cross-roads we found the master of the Esker hunt, a big, wild-looking man with a long reddish-grey beard and a moustache, seated on an ugly yellow horse with a black stripe, like a donkey's, down his back.

" How do you do, Mr. Dennehy ? " said Willy, as we rode up. " Nice day. This is my cousin, Miss Sarsfield. I hope you'll show her some sport. Morning, Nugent. How are you, Miss Connie ? Do you see the new mount I have ? " and Willy forgot his duties as my chaperon, in congenial conversation with Miss O'Neill.

Mr. Dennehy, with what was, I believe, unwonted condescension, began to speak to me.

" I'm delighted to see you out, Miss Sarsfield," he said in a slow, solemn brogue. " I hope we'll have a good day for you, and if there's a fox in Clashmore at all, these little hounds of mine will have him out."

I did not know much about hounds, but even to inexperienced eyes these appeared to be a very motley collection. Mr. Dennehy saw me look with interest at two strange little dogs, somewhat resembling long-legged black-and-tan terriers.

" Well, Miss Sarsfield, those are the two best hounds I have, though they're ugly creatures enough. And there's a good hound. Loo, Solomon, good hound ! That's a hound will only spake to game."

Here Mr. Dennehy produced a battered little horn, and with two or three bleats upon it to collect his hounds, he put the yellow horse at a yawning black ditch that divided the road from a narrow strip of rough ground, perpendicularly from which rose a steep hill covered with laurels. The yellow horse took the ditch and the low stone wall on its farther side with unassuming skill, and he and Mr. Dennehy were presently lost to sight in the wood.

Willy now came up to me with Miss O'Neill and her brother, and I was introduced to the former, a small, fair-haired girl in a smart habit, with brown eyes and a high colour. She nodded to me with cheery indifference, and continued her conversation with Willy, leaving me to talk to her brother.

This I found to be a somewhat difficult task. His manner was exceedingly polite, but he appeared to be engrossed in watching the covert, and we finally relapsed into silence. At intervals Mr. Dennehy's red coat showed between the low close-growing trees as he led his horse through the covert, and we could hear his original method of encouraging his hounds.

"Thatsy me darlins! Thatsy-atsy-atsy! Turrn him out, Woodbine! Hi, Waurior, good hound!"

I felt inclined to laugh, but as no one else seemed amused, I concluded that this was classical "hound-language" and waited respectfully for further developments. Presently, with a few words to Willy, Mr. O'Neill put spurs to his bay horse and galloped off. In a moment or two, Miss O'Neill, without further ceremony, followed her brother to the other end of the covert, and Willy and I remained with about twenty other riders on the road.

"See here!" he said in low, excited tones. "You keep close to me. Old Dennehy's got a beastly trick of slipping away with his hounds directly they find, and making fools of the whole field, leaving them the wrong side of the covert. But I think we're in a good place here. Whisht! wasn't that a hound speaking? Come on this way."

We clattered down the road helter-skelter, but were stopped by an excited rush of country boys with shouts of, "He's gone aisht! He's broke the far side!" and at the same instant Mr. and Miss O'Neill came pounding down a ride out of the covert.

"It's just as I thought: Dennehy's gone away with the hounds by himself," called out Mr. O'Neill. "A country fellow saw the fox heading for Braad, and Dennehy all alone with the hounds, going like mad!"

At this juncture I think it better not to record Willy's comments.

"It's all right, Nugent," said Connie, whirling her

mare round. " I know a way over the hill lower
down."

" Don't mind her, Theo," said Willy in my ear ;
" just you stick to me."

We had galloped past the eastern bound of the
wood, and as he spoke he turned his horse and
jumped the fence on the right of the road. Blackthorn followed of his own accord, and I found that
an Irish bank did not feel as difficult as it looked.

Willy turned in his saddle to watch me.

" Well done ! that's your sort," he shouted.
" Hold him now, and hit him ! This is a big place
we're coming to."

We were over before I had time to think, and to my
horror I saw that Willy was making for a hill that
looked like the side of a house, covered with furze.

" There's a way up here, but you'll have to lead.
Nip off ! I'll go first."

I was fearfully out of breath, but Willy allowed no
time for delay. Up the hill we scrambled, Blackthorn
leading me considerably more than I led him. After
the first few seconds of climbing, I felt as if it would
be impossible to go on. My habit hindered me at
every step. Blackthorn's jerks and tugs at the reins
nearly threw me on my face, and the fear of Willy
alone prevented me from letting him finish the ascent
by himself. When at last we reached the top, Willy
and I were both so much out of breath that we could
not speak, and I wished for nothing so much as to lie
down and have apoplexy comfortably. But Willy,
with a blazing face, made signs to me to mount at

once, and, jerking me into the saddle, we again set off.

The top of the hill which we had now gained was rough, boggy ground. Down to our right lay the gleaming laurel covert, and in front of us the hill sloped gradually down into a low tract of bog and lakes, with hills beyond. We could see nothing of any one, but a countryman, on the top of a bank above the wood, waved semaphore-like directions that the hounds were running to the north-east.

" Hullo ! here's Nugent," said Willy, in a not over-pleased voice, and as he spoke I saw Mr. O'Neill's bay horse coming along over the hill. He soon overtook us, looking, I was glad to see, as heated and dishevelled as Willy and I.

" I knew that way of Connie's was no use, so I came back and went up the hill after you. Where are the hounds ? "

" Going north-east, a fellow told me. Look ! Look at the brutes ! There they are on the hill across the bog, going straight for Braad ! "

" There's only one way to pick them up," said Nugent, with what seemed to me unnatural calm— " we must cross the bog."

" The bog is it ? " echoed Willy. " Try it if you like, but if you once get in you'll not get out in a hurry ! "

" Do you mind trying, Miss Sarsfield ? " demanded Mr. O'Neill.

" Whatever Willy likes," I said, diplomatically.

"Oh, all right," said Willy. "Fire away, but you'll have to pay for the funeral, Nugent."

We had now reached the foot of the hill, and we galloped along the verge of the bog for a short distance till we came to where a broad and broken bank traversed it in a north-easterly direction.

"Here's the place. If we can get along the top of this, we might just hit them off," Mr. O'Neill said. He went first, and the horses picked their way along the top of the bank like cats, though the sides crumbled under their feet, and sometimes the whole structure tottered as if it were going to collapse into the deep dykes on either side. At last it broke sharp off, at a pool of black mire. Our guide dismounted and jumped down into the bog, pulling his horse after him, and we slowly dragged our way through the heavy ground to the farther side of the bog.

Here we were confronted by the most formidable obstacle we had yet come to. It consisted of a low, soft-looking bank, with a wide boggy ditch beyond it.

"We've got to try it, I suppose," said Willy, "but it's a thundering big jump, and there's a deuced bad landing beyond the water."

He and Mr. O'Neill remounted, and the latter put his horse at the place. The bay's hoofs sank deep in the bank, but he made an effort that landed him safely on the opposite side on comparatively firm ground. My turn came next.

"Whip him over it!" exclaimed Willy.

I did so as well as I was able, but the treacherous

ground broke under Blackthorn's feet, and he all but floundered back into the ditch as he landed.

" Oh, Willy ! " I cried, " I'm afraid you'll never get her over now that the bank is broken."

But Willy was already too much occupied with Alaska to make any reply. She refused several times ; finally, yielding to the inevitable, she threw herself rather than jumped off the bank, and the next moment she and Willy were in the ditch.

I was terrified as to the consequences, and was much relieved when I saw Willy, black from head to foot, crawl from the mare's back on to the more solid mud of the bank on our side. Without a word he caught Alaska by the head, and began to try and pull her out. His extraordinary appearance, and the fact that he was much too angry to be in the least conscious of its absurdity, had the disastrous effect of reducing both Mr. O'Neill and me to heartless laughter.

" I am very sorry, Willy," I panted, " and I am delighted you're not hurt ; but if you could only see yourself ! "

Willy silently continued his efforts.

" Oh, Mr. O'Neill, do get down and help him," I continued.

" I don't want any help, thank you," returned my cousin, with restrained fury. " Come up out of that, you brute ! "—applying his hunting-crop with vigour to the recumbent Alaska, who thereupon, with two or three violent efforts, heaved herself out of the slough. All this time Mr. O'Neill had been grinning with that unfeigned delight which all hunting-men seem to derive from the misfortunes of their friends.

"You have toned down that new coat, Willy," he remarked ; "and I must say the little mare takes to water like an otter."

"Oh, I dare say it's very funny indeed ! " retorted Willy, leading Alaska on to the higher ground where we were standing ; "but if you'd an eye in your head you'd see the mare is dead lame."

"By George ! so she is. That's hard luck. She must have given herself a strain."

"Well, whatever ails her, there's no use in your standing there looking at me," replied Willy. "I can get home all right. I don't want Theo to lose the run, and you'll head them yet if you put on the pace."

His magnanimity was almost more crushing than his wrath. I was filled with contrition, and begged to be allowed to stay with him. But I was given no voice in the matter ; my offer was scouted, and before I had fairly grasped the situation I was galloping up a narrow mountain road after Nugent O'Neill.

CHAPTER X.

After we had gone about a quarter of a mile, my companion pulled up.

"I think our best chance is to wait here," he said. "From the way the hounds were running, they are bound to come this way."

The road up which we had ridden formed the only pass between the hills on either side of us, and beyond was a low-lying level stretch of country.

"If he'll only run down that way——" Mr. O'Neill began, but suddenly stopped, and silently pointed with his whip to the hill at our right.

"What is it?" I asked, in incautiously loud tones.

He looked for an instant as if he were going to shake his whip at me, and again pointed, this time to a narrow strip of field beside the road. I saw what looked like a little brown shadow fleeting across it, and in another moment the fox appeared on the top of the wall a few yards ahead of us. He looked about him as if considering his next move, and then, seeing us, he leaped into the road, and, running along it, vanished over the crest of the hill.

Mr. O'Neill turned to me with such excitement

that he seemed a different person. "Here are the hounds!" he said, "and not a soul with them!"

Down the hill the pack came like a torrent, and were over the wall in a second. They spread themselves over the road in front of us as if at fault; but one of the little black-and-tans justified Mr. Dennehy's good opinion by picking up the line, and at once the whole pack were racing full cry up the road.

I have often looked back with considerable amusement to that moment. I was suddenly possessed by a kind of frenzy of excitement that deprived me of all power of speech. I heard my companion tell me to keep as close to him as I could, but I was incapable of any response save an inebriated smile and a wholly absurd flourish of my whip.

As this does not purport to be a hunting story, I will not describe the run which followed. I believe it lasted fifteen minutes, and included some of the traditional "big leps" of the country. But to me it was merely an indefinite period of delirious happiness. I scarcely felt Blackthorn jump, and was only conscious of the thud of the big bay horse's hoofs in front of me and the rushing of the wind in my ears. At last a wood seemed to heave up before me; the bay horse was pulled up sharply, and I found myself almost in the middle of the hounds.

"By George! he's just saved his brush," said Mr. O'Neill, breathlessly; "he's gone to ground in there, and we'll never get him out. I hope you are none the worse for your gallop," he continued politely. "It was pretty fast while it lasted." He dismounted as he spoke, and began to investigate the hole in which the fox had taken refuge, and while he was thus engaged I saw Mr. Dennehy on his yellow horse coming across the next field. When he came up he was, rather to my surprise, amiably pleased at our success in picking up the hounds, and regretted we had not killed our fox.

" You two and meself were the only ones in this run," he said.

My thoughts at once reverted to poor Willy. I asked Mr. Dennehy if he had seen anything of him, and heard that he had passed my cousin, slowly making his way home.

" Oh, I think I ought to go home at once," I said to Mr. O'Neill. " I might overtake him if you will tell me where I am to go."

" If you will allow me, I think you had better let me show you the way," he answered, with a resumption of the stiff manner which had at first struck me. It was only too obvious that politeness alone had prompted this offer, but my ignorance of the country made it impossible for me to refuse it. I could but hope that by speedily overtaking Willy I should be able to release my unwilling pilot, and with affectionate farewells from Mr. Dennehy, we proceeded to make the best of our way to the nearest road.

Our way lay through what seemed to me a chessboard of absurdly small fields. I could not imagine where all the stones came from that were squandered in the heaping up of the walls that divided them from each other, nor did I greatly care, so long as the necessity of jumping them gave me something to amuse me, and made conversation with Mr. O'Neill disjointed and unexacting.

What little I had seen of him at the covert-side had not inspired me with any anxiety to pursue his acquaintance, and once we had got out on to the road, with all the responsibilities of a *tête-à-tête* staring us in the face, my heart died within me. Never had I met any one who was so difficult to talk to. I found that I was gradually assuming the ungrateful position of a catechist, and, while filled with smothered indignation at my companion's perfunctory answers, I could not repress a certain admiration for the composure with which he allowed the whole stress of discourse to rest upon my shoulders. I at length made up my mind to give myself no more trouble in the cause of politeness, and resolved that until he chose to speak I would not do so.

A long silence was the result. We rode on side by side, my companion staring steadily between his horse's ears, while I wondered how soon we should be likely to meet Willy, and thought how very much more I should have preferred his society.

" I suppose you find this place rather dull ? " Mr. O'Neill's uninterested voice at last broke the silence. " I have always heard that Canadian young ladies had a very gay time."

I at once felt that this insufferably old young man was trying to talk down to my level—the level of a " Canadian young lady "—and my smouldering resentment got the better of my politeness.

" I very seldom find myself bored by places. It is, as a rule, the people of the place that bore me."

" Really," he returned, with perfect serenity. " Yes, I dare say that is true ; but ladies do not generally get on very well without shops and dances."

" Strange as it may appear, neither of those entrancing occupations is essential to my happiness."

I felt this to be very crushing. So, apparently, did Mr. O'Neill, for he turned and looked at me with faint surprise, but made no reply. Another pause ensued, and I began to repent of my crossness.

It was clearly my turn to make the next remark, and I said, in a more conciliatory voice—

" I suppose you don't have very much to do here, either ? "

" Oh, I am not here very much, and I can always get as much shooting and fishing as I want ; but I fancy my sisters find it rather dull."

" Are your sisters fond of music ?   I was very glad to find a piano at Durrus."

His face assumed for the first time a look of interest.

" My eldest sister plays a good deal ; and Connie has a banjo, though I can't say she knows much about it ; and I play the fiddle a little.   I believe in these parts we are considered quite a gifted family."

I felt that I had, so to speak, " struck ile."

" Do you play the violin ? " I said, with excitement.   " I delight in playing accompaniments !   I hope you will bring your music with you when you come to dinner."

"Oh, thanks very much; my sister always accompanies me," he responded coolly.

His deliberate self-possession was infinitely exasperating in my then state of mind, and I repented the enthusiasm that had laid me open to this snub. I was hurriedly framing an effective rejoinder, when he again spoke, this time in tones of considerable amusement.

"Do you see that man leading a lame horse down the road? He may be a chimney-sweep, but I am inclined to think it is Willy."

As we came nearer, I was secretly unspeakably tickled by Willy's inky and bedraggled appearance; but I was too proud to join in Mr. O'Neill's open amusement, until I noticed for the first time the incongruously rakish effect imparted to Willy's forlorn figure by the fact that his hat had been crushed in. My injured dignity collapsed, and, holding on to my saddle for support, I laughed till the tears poured down my cheeks.

It was at this singularly unpropitious moment that Willy, hearing our horses' feet, turned round.

"Oh, there you are!" he called out. "Did you meet the hounds?" Then, in a voice which showed his good temper had not returned, "You seem to be greatly amused, whatever you did."

I thought it better to ignore the latter part of the sentence, and dashed at once into a confused account of our exploits, Mr. O'Neill helping out my narrative with a few geographical details; to all of which Willy listened with morose attention.

"And Blackthorn jumped splendidly, Willy," I said. "I was so sorry you weren't there."

"H'm!" said Willy; "very sorry indeed, I've no doubt!"

Mr. O'Neill saw that the situation was becoming strained.

"As I can't be of any further help to you or Miss Sarsfield," he said, "I think I will go back and look for the hounds;" and, wishing us good-bye, he rode off.

"Well," Willy began viciously, "you seem to find O'Neill cheerful enough, after all."

"*Indeed* I don't, Willy," I said, with vigour; "he was perfectly *odious*."

"You didn't look as if you thought him so a while ago, when you were both near falling off your horses with laughing. I suppose"—with sudden penetration—"that it was at me you were laughing."

"Oh no, Willy; at least, it was not exactly you—indeed, it was only your hat."

Even at this supreme moment the air of disreputable gaiety of Willy's headgear was too much for me, and my voice broke into an hysterical shriek. This was the last straw. With a wrathful glance, he turned his back upon me, and stalked silently on beside Alaska. Blackthorn and I followed meekly in the rear, and in this order we sombrely proceeded to Durrus.

CHAPTER XI.

A LOWERING grey sky succeeded the sunshine of the day of the hunt. I crawled down late to breakfast, feeling agonisingly stiff after the previous day's exertions, and was on the whole relieved to find that Willy had gone out for a long day's shooting, and that till lunch at least I should have no one to entertain but myself.

The evening before had been, as far as Willy had been concerned, of a rather complicated type. I had done all in my power to efface from his mind the memory of my unfortunate laughter, but until dinner was over he had remained implacable. Uncle Dominick, on the contrary, had been unusually bland and talkative. It appeared that Madam O'Neill and her eldest daughter had called on me while I was out, and my uncle, having met them on the drive, had brought them in, given them tea, and had even gone so far as to ask the two girls to come with their brother to dinner the next night. He had given me to understand that this unusual hospitality was on my account—" Although," he added, " I have no doubt you two young people are quite well able to amuse each other." The look which accompanied this was, under the circumstances, so peculiarly embarrassing, that, in order to change the conversation, I made the mistake of beginning to describe the hunt. Too soon I discovered that to slur over Willy's disaster would be impossible, and my obvious efforts to do so did not improve matters.

" So you went off with young O'Neill," my uncle had said, with a change of look and voice that frightened me ; and nothing more was said on the subject.

My discomfiture was perhaps the cause of the alteration in Willy's demeanour after dinner. Success far beyond my expectations, or indeed my wishes, was the result of my conciliatory advances. I went to bed feeling that I had more than regained the position I had held in Willy's esteem, and a little flurried by the difficulties of so ambiguous a relationship as that of first cousins.

From all this, it may be imagined that when I heard from Roche that " the masther was gone to town, and would not be home for lunch," I regarded the combined absences of Willy and his father as little short of providential.

I observed that the magenta and yellow dahlias which had decorated the table on my arrival still held their ground, albeit in an advanced stage of decay ; and, remembering the glories of the autumn leaves, I suggested to Roche that with his permission I might be able to improve upon the present arrangement.

A little elated by the expectation of surprising

Willy with the unusual splendour of the dinner-table, and not without an emulative thought of the O'Neills, I determined to ransack the shrubberies for the most glowing leaves wherewith to carry out my purpose. A few minutes later I left the house with a capacious basket in my hand, feeling a delightful sense of freedom, and full of the buccaneering pleasure of a solitary and irresponsible voyage of discovery.

I wandered down the nearest path to the sea, and, keeping to the shore, came to the little promontory which, with its few ragged trees, I could see from the windows of my room. There was a romance about this lonely wind- and wave-beaten point that from the first had appealed to me. When, in the early light, I saw the fir-trees' weird reflection in the quiet cove I used to wonder if they had ever been a landmark for some western Dick Hatteraick ; and now, as I scrambled about, and tugged at the tough bramble-stems that trailed in the coarse grass, I was half-persuaded that any one of the rough boulders might close the entrance of a smuggler's long-forgotten " hide."

I had soon gathered as many blackberry leaves as I wanted, and, sitting down beside one of the old trees, I leaned my cheek against its seamy trunk and looked across the grey rollers to the horizon.

A narrow black line stole from behind the eastern point of Durrusmore Harbour, leaving a dark stain on the sky as it went, and from where I sat I could hear the beat of machinery.

It was the first time I had noticed the passing of one of the big American steamers, and I watched the great creature move out of sight with a strange conflict of feeling. Uppermost, I think, was the thought of what my regret would be if I were at that moment on board her, bound for America. I was a little ashamed when I reflected how soon the newer interests had superseded the old. I had been but a week in Ireland, and already the idea of leaving it was akin to that of emigration. What, I wondered, was the charm that had worked so quickly ? Was this subtle familiarity and satisfaction with my new life merely the result of æsthetic interest, or had it the depth of an inherited instinct ?

I could not tell ; I could only feel a strange presentiment that my existence had hitherto been nothing but a preface, and that I was now on the threshold of what was to be, for good or evil, my real life.

I picked up my basket and retraced my steps down the little slope, till I again found myself in the shrubbery walk. On one point my mind was clear. My liking for Durrus was in no perceptible degree influenced by my feeling for my uncle and my cousin. I reiterated this to myself as I strolled along in the damp shade of overarching laurels towards the plantation which lay between the sea and the lodge.

Uncle Dominick was anything but a person to inspire immediate affection ; and then Willy—well, Willy certainly had many attractive points, but, although he was a pleasant companion, he could not be said to be either very cultured or refined.

I left the path and strayed through the wood, stopping here and there to rob the branches of their lavish autumn loveliness. A sluggish little stream crept among the trees, and along its banks the ferns grew thickly. I knelt down in the stubbly yellow grass beside it, where the pale trunk of a beech-tree stooped over the water, and picked the small delicate ferns that were clustering between its roots. Having gathered all within reach, I still knelt there, watching a little procession of withered beech-leaves making their slow way down the stream, and studying my own dark reflection on the water.

I was at length startled by the sound of voices that seemed to come from the path I had just left, but from where I was, the thickness of the intervening laurels prevented me from seeing to whom they belonged.

It soon became evident that one of the speakers was a country girl. She was talking rapidly and earnestly; but what she said was unintelligible to me till she and her companion came to the point in the path which was nearest to me, when, after a momentary pause, the soft voice broke out—

" Ye won't lave me for her, will ye, now ? Ye *said* ye'd hold by me always, and now——"

Something between a sob and a choke ended the sentence. Several sobs followed ; and then the girl's voice went on excitedly—

" Ah ! 'tis no use your goin' on like that ; ye know ye want to have done with me entirely."

I could hear no reply ; but that reassurance and consolation were offered was obvious, for as the footsteps died away I heard something like a broken laugh from the girl, with some faint echo of it from a man's voice.

" Who can she be ? " I thought, compassionately. There was a perplexing familiarity in the low pathetic voice, and I walked home, feeling unnecessarily depressed and troubled by what I had heard, and wondering with all the self-righteousness of inexperience at the self-abandonment which had led to such an appeal.

The path by which I returned skirted the garden and formed a loop with the one by which I had first entered the wood. As I approached the broader walk, I saw a girl's figure flit down the other path, and I had just time to recognise it as being that of Anstey Brian. Simultaneously came the recollection of the pleading voice in the wood, and in an instant I knew why it had been familiar.

" Then it must have been Anstey," I thought, feeling both sorry and startled. The entreaty in her voice had made it very plain how serious a matter her trouble was to her, and the helplessness of her quick surrender showed that she had lost all power of resistance or resentment. I was astonished to think that so pretty a girl as Anstey should have cause to reproach her sweetheart with want of constancy. " Who could he be ? " I wondered. Then,

remembering that the path she was on was a usual
short cut from the lodge to the yard, I came to the
conclusion that one of the Durrus stablemen must
have been the object of that broken-hearted appeal.
I determined that I would try and find out something further about Anstey and her lover, and wondered if it would be of any use to mention the subject
to Willy.

CHAPTER XII.

IN spite of the incontestable success of my decorations, which drew forth the admiration of even the superior Henrietta O'Neill, I felt, before we had arrived at the period of fish, that the dinner-party was likely to be a failure.

Uncle Dominick had, of course, taken in the elder Miss O'Neill, and as far as they were concerned nothing was left to be desired. Conversation of a fluent and high-class order was evidently her strong point. She at once entered upon a discussion of Irish politics with my uncle in a manner deserving of all praise, and as I surreptitiously studied her pale, plain, intellectual face, with the dark hair severely drawn back, and heard her enunciate her opinions in clearly framed sentences, I became deeply conscious of my own general inferiority.

Nevertheless, I did what in me lay to talk to Nugent O'Neill, who had taken me in, thus leaving to Willy the necessary and, as I thought, congenial task of entertaining Miss Connie. Nothing could apparently be better arranged. Nugent had exchanged his frigid, uninterested civility of the day before for an excellent semblance of sociability, beneath which, as it seemed to me, he concealed a curious observation of all that I said. He had a dark clever face, strong well-cut features, and blue eyes, with a pleasanter expression in them than I had at first expected to see there. His voice would have been monotonous in its quietness and unexcitability had it not been for a certain humorous turn which now and then made its way into his sentences. He annoyed me, but at the same time he was interesting; moreover—which was to me a very strong point in his favour—he was evidently as much alive as I to the fact that for the next hour and a half it would be our solemn duty to amuse each other, and to that intent we both performed prodigies of agreeability.

But Willy was the cause of disaster. I became gradually aware that silence was settling down upon him and Connie, and that, instead of devoting himself to her, he, with his eyes fixed on me and my partner, was listening moodily to what we were saying. When this had gone on for some minutes, during which Connie crumbled her bread and looked cross, I was exasperated to the point of bestowing a glance upon him calculated to awaken in him a sense of his bad manners. Far, however, from accepting my reproof, Willy returned my look with a gaze of admiring defiance, and projected himself into our conversation by flatly contradicting what Nugent was saying. The latter rose many degrees in my estimation by ignoring the interruption till he had reached the end of his sentence. Then, with a tolerating smile, he

looked past me to Willy, and asked him what he had
said.

Willy's dark eyebrows met in a way that un-
pleasantly reminded me of his father.

" If it wasn't worth listening to, it's not worth
repeating," he said aggressively.

Terrified by the turn things were taking, I struck
in quickly, " Oh, Willy ! have you told Miss O'Neill
what you heard to-day about the Jackson-Crolys
giving a ball ? "

" No ; I thought she'd have heard it herself," he
returned ungraciously.

" As it happens, I had heard nothing about it," said
Connie, from the other side of the table ; " but I cannot say that I feel much excited at the prospect of
one of their dances."

" I am looking forward to it immensely," I said,
persevering with my topic. " I want very much to
see a real Irish ball."

" Yes," said Nugent, reflectively, " you will see
that at the Jackson-Crolys'. They excel in old Irish
hospitality. They do that kind of thing in quite
the traditional way. Little Croly offers you whisky
the moment you get into the hall : and Mrs. Jackson-
Croly orders champagne to be put into all the carriages when people are coming away. The guests
are generally pretty happy by that time, and she says
it is to keep their hearts up on the way home."

" That's quite true," observed Connie ; " and, as
well as I remember, you were not at all above drinking it next day."

"Do they dance jigs at these entertainments?" I asked. "If so, I am afraid I shall be rather out of it."

"Oh yes," said Willy, with what was intended to be biting sarcasm; "and hornpipes and Highland flings. They always do at Irish dances."

"Nonsense, Willy! They don't really, do they, Mr. O'Neill?"

"It is always well to be prepared for emergencies," he answered, "so I should advise you to have some lessons from Willy. I have been told that step-dancing is his strong suit."

"Who told you that?" demanded Willy.

"One of our men was at McCarthy's wedding the other day, and said he saw you there."

"Oh yes," supplemented Connie. "He said, 'The sight would have your eyes to see Mr. Sarsfield and that little gerr'l of owld Michael Brian's taking the flure, and they so souple and so springy.'"

Willy did not appear to be at all amused by this flattering opinion, or by the admirable accent in which it was repeated. On the contrary, he looked rather disconcerted, and, with a glance towards the other end of the table, he said awkwardly—

"Oh, one has to do these sort of things now and then. The people like it, and it doesn't do me any harm."

"On the contrary," said Nugent, "I am sure it is a most healthy exercise. But I thought it rather spoiled your leg for a top-boot."

Willy was known to favour knee-breeches as being

especially becoming to him, and at this, to my great relief, he turned his back upon us, and plunged into an ostentatiously engrossing conversation with Connie. At last we were in smooth water, and with almost a sigh of relief I heard Nugent take up the thread of our discourse at the point where Willy had broken it off.

It was evident that he could be pleasant enough when he chose ; and though I felt that this new development was almost as offensive in another way as his deliberate dullness yesterday, I was now very grateful for its timely help. At the same time, I bore in mind with resentment my unremunerated toil during our ride, and reflected bitterly on the fact that people who only talk when it pleases them, receive far more credit when they do so than those who from a sense of duty exhaust themselves conversationally.

Uncle Dominick and Henrietta had up to this not caused me a moment's anxiety. We were now at dessert, and yet the flow of their discourse had never flagged. In fact, my uncle seemed at present to be delivering a species of harangue, to which Henrietta was attending with a polite unconvinced smile. This was all as it should be, and my respect for Henrietta's social gifts increased tenfold. Unfortunately, however, it soon became evident that the discussion, whatever it was, was taking rather too personal a tone, and my uncle's voice became so loud and overbearing that Nugent and I were constrained to listen to him.

" You amaze me," he was saying. " I cannot

believe that any sane person can honestly hold such absurd theories. What ! do you mean to tell me that one of my tenants, a creature whose forefathers have lived for centuries in ignorance and degradation, is my equal ? "

" His degradation is merely the result of injustice," said Miss O'Neill, coolly adjusting her *pince-nez*.

" I deny it," said my uncle, loudly. His usually pale face was flushed, and his eyes burned. " But that is not the point. What I maintain is, that any fusion of classes such as you advocate would have the effect of debasing the upper while it entirely failed to raise the lower orders. If you were to marry your coachman, as, according to your theories of equality, I suppose you would not hesitate to do, do you think these latent instincts of refinement that you talk about would make him a fit companion for you and your family ? You know as well as I do that such an idea is preposterous. It is absurd to suppose that the natural arrangement of things can be tampered with. This is a subject on which I feel very strongly, and it shocks me to hear a young lady in your position advance such opinions ! "

Henrietta's face assumed an aggravating expression, clearly conveying her opinion that further argument would be thrown away. Uncle Dominick gulped down a glass of wine, and glared round the table. There was a general silence, and I took advantage of it to make a move to the drawing-room.

I was wholly taken aback by my uncle's violence, and could not help fearing that the number of times

4

his glass had been replenished had had something to say to it. Willy's temper had also been so uncertain that I dreaded an outbreak between him and his father, and, in the interval of waiting for their reappearance, I found myself making the most absent and ill-chosen answers to Henrietta's questions upon the culture and political status of Canadian women, while I listened anxiously for the sound of the opening of the dining-room door. My only consolation was that Nugent would, for his own sake, do his best to keep the peace, and I was surprised to find how much I relied on his powers of doing so.

In my preoccupied state of mind, it is not to be wondered at that Henrietta soon appeared to come to the conclusion that I was incapable of giving her any information on the subjects in which she was interested, and that I was generally a person of limited abilities. She leaned back in her chair with the exhausted air of one who relinquishes a hopeless task, and, taking up a photograph-book, she tacitly made me over to her sister.

Connie's ideas ran in less exalted grooves. The run of the day before was to her a topic of inexhaustible interest ; and when she found that my humility in the matter of hunting equalled my ignorance, she expanded into extreme graciousness, and was soon in the full tide of narration. The story-teller who treats of hunting with any real enthusiasm generally loses all mental perspective, and sacrifices artistic unity to historical accuracy. Then, as now, I was amazed at the powers of memory and merciless fidelity to detail with which those who have taken part in a run can afterwards describe it, and I listened with reverence befitting the neophyte to Connie's adventures by flood and field. Foxes and fences, hounds and hunters, were revolving in my brain, when the opening of the door brought the story to a conclusion, and Willy came into the room, followed by Nugent. He marched directly to the sofa where I was sitting, and deposited himself beside me with such determination that the rebound of its springs almost lifted me into the air.

This behaviour was really intolerable. Willy had not before shown any very pronounced partiality for me, and why he should have selected this evening for a demonstration of affection it would be hard to say. One thing was clear: it must be suppressed with a strong hand, or a deadlock would ensue. Nugent was standing on the hearthrug, with apparently no prospect of entertainment before him save what he could derive from talking to his sisters ; while those two young ladies were well aware that no reasonable hostess could ask them to dinner and expect them to devote their evening to conversing with their brother, and, pending action on my part, were sitting in expectant silence. I turned upon Willy in desperation.

" You *must* talk to them," I hissed in his ear.

To which, with equal emphasis, he whispered back, " I won't ! " fixing upon me a blandly stubborn gaze that infuriated me beyond the bounds of endurance.

I leaped from my seat, and, with a timely recollection of Nugent's violin, I walked over to him and asked if he had remembered to bring it. He admitted apologetically that it was in the hall, adding, with unexpected modesty, that he had only brought it because I had asked him to do so. I had some acquaintance with the ways of amateur violinists, and speedily recognised the diffidence which conceals a yearning to play at all hazards. My intention to dislike him was softened by the discovery that he was not at all points so superior as I had believed, and I was pleased to notice some hurry and trepidation in his manner while he was tuning his violin. Henrietta advanced upon the piano with an air of sisterly resignation, and, concealing a yawn, tapped a note for Nugent to tune by.

While he was thus engaged, I cast an anxious eye round the room. My uncle had now come in, and, with his elbow on the chimney-piece, was looking into the fire. Connie had taken possession of the ancient photograph-book which her sister had put down, and, in company with Willy, was silently and methodically turning over its yellow pages. Well did I know its contents. Ladies in preposterously inflated skirts, with rows of black velvet round the tail ; and gentlemen clad from head to heel in decent black, each with his back to an Italian landscape, and his tall hat on a Grecian pedestal near him—all alike undistinguishable and unknown. I felt sincerely for Connie ; but other occupation there was none, and I had done my best on her behalf.

I was at first inclined to agree with Nugent in his own estimate of his playing, and I saw with unworthy amusement that he was extremely nervous ; but as he went on he steadied down, and played with sweetness, and with what was almost more surprising, sentiment. The keen notes vibrated in the dim, lofty room, and tingled in the many hanging crystals of the old glass chandelier. I forgot the indignation which he had yesterday aroused in me, and remained leaning on the piano, conscious only of the pleasure I was receiving, until the player ceased, and began to unscrew his bow preparatory to putting it away.

"Please play something else," I said hastily. "Won't you try this Suite of Corelli's ? I know it so well."

"I am afraid my sister doesn't know the accompaniment," he answered, with a dubious look at Henrietta, who was rising from the piano.

Her bored manner had already told me that she looked on accompanying her brother as a task beneath her powers, and the thought struck me with paralysing conviction that I ought to have asked her to play a solo. However, this was not the moment to rectify the error ; Nugent was lingering over the putting away of his violin, with an obvious desire to play again.

"I suppose it would be too much to ask you to try it ? " he said to me, after another glance at Henrietta's unresponsive face.

"Perhaps if it was not very difficult I might be able——" I said, and checked myself, remembering the snub I had received on that very subject.

But now that I had admitted so much, Nugent

held me to my word, and firmly proceeded to arrange the piano part on the desk for me.

"I don't envy you, Miss Sarsfield," remarked Henrietta, with a cold little laugh; "Nugent's ideas of counting are excessively primitive."

Decidedly Henrietta was annoyed.

"I am the class of savage who cannot count more than five," he replied, addressing me; "but I do my best."

Miss O'Neill laughed again. "You will have to play it for him," she said, moving away from the piano; "Nugent is a regular bully."

We played the piece I had asked for, as well as several others, before I remembered my duties as hostess. Willy had forsaken Connie and the photograph-book, and had again left her and Henrietta to talk to each other, while he propped himself against the chimney-piece, and gazed moodily at Nugent and me.

I could not have believed that he would have left me in this dastardly way to bear the burden and heat of the entertainment, and I made a second effort to keep things going by begging Miss O'Neill to play. But this time I was unsuccessful; she would not be propitiated. A look passed between her and her sister, whose banjo I now had little doubt had been secreted in the hall; while I, in violation of all the laws of civility, had myself been monopolising the piano. They both got up from their places.

"I should have been delighted," said Henrietta, "but I am afraid it is getting rather late. My dear

Nugent "—calling to her brother, who was carefully swaddling his violin preparatory to putting it away—" we really ought to be getting home. The carriage must have been waiting some time ; and I am sure " —in a lower voice—" that Mr. Sarsfield has had quite enough of us."

I looked at my uncle, who during the violin-playing had sunk into an arm-chair, and had shaded his eyes with his hand, as if listening attentively. He had not moved since we stopped, and looked almost as if he were asleep ; but there was something in his attitude that conveyed the idea of deep dejection rather than of slumber.

The general stir of departure roused him. He rose slowly, and said good-night with a little more than his usual gloom.

CHAPTER XIII.

ONE day at Durrus was very like another. By the time I had been there three weeks or a month, the days stretched out behind me into indefinite length, separating me more and more from my past life.

Looking back to that time, it seems to resolve itself into one long *tête-à-tête* with Willy. Quiet rides with him through the damp brown woods, or now and then a day with the Esker hounds; drives to return the visits of such of the natives as had called upon me; walks across the turf bog to where the old graveyard hung over the sea, to watch the sun drop below the horizon. "Bound for America," says Willy. "I wonder if you'd like to be going back with him?" I had no doubts in my own mind on the subject, though I did not feel called upon to say so to him. I was now quite certain that, in spite of various drawbacks, I enjoyed my life at Durrus very much.

I have said that I had had callers. After the O'Neills, among the first to come and see me were Mrs. Jackson-Croly and her daughters, the Burkes, whose acquaintance I had already made, and Mrs. Barrett, a monumental old lady, who having been established by Willy in the most reliable chair in the room, remained there in mammoth silence, motionless, save for her alert eyes, which wandered from face to face, and suggested to me the idea of a restless intelligent spirit imprisoned in a feather bed.

The imposing voice of Mrs. Jackson-Croly dominated the room.

" Yes, Miss Sarsfield," she said, " I'm thinking of taking the girls to Southsea. There's such nice military society there. I always like to take them to England as often as I can, on account of the accent. I loathe a Cork brogue ! My fawther took me abroad every year ; he was so alormed lest I'd acquire it, and I assure you, when we were children, he used to insist on mamma's putting cotton wool in our ears when we went to old Mr. Flannagan's church, for fear we'd ketch his manner of speaking."

" Dear, dear ! " said Miss Burke, sympathetically. " Poor old Johnny Flannagan ! He had a beautiful voice in the pulpit. I declare "—turning to me— " sometimes you'd think the people out in the street would hear him, and the next minute you'd think 'twas a pigeon cooing to you ! "

It would have been pleasant to have led Miss Burke on to further reminiscences of this gifted divine, but another and more exciting topic presented itself to her.

" Oh Miss Sarsfield ! and what's this we hear about you and Mr. O'Neill ? Springing away through the country after the fox, and leaving poor Willy in the ditch ! Oh fie ! "

I feel that it is hopeless to convey an adequate idea of Miss Mimi's voice by any system of spelling. It must be enough to mention that " fie " she pronounced " foy," and " Sarsfield " in her sonorous tones became " Sorsefield."

The eyes of Mrs. Barrett rolled upon me speechlessly, and those of Mrs. Jackson-Croly and her two daughters were fixed upon me with such an access of interest that I hastened to explain how it was that Willy had been left behind. My unadorned narrative fell singularly flat, and Miss Burke broached another theme that came as a magnum of champagne after my small beer.

" Well, Mrs. Croly, and is it true that you are going to give us a dance at Mount Prospect ? " she began. " Why, you're a grand woman ! we'd all be dying down with dulness only for you ! "

Mrs. Jackson-Croly, metaphorically speaking, descended with one leap from the pedestal on which she had hitherto posed for my benefit. She dragged her chair, still seated upon it, across the floor, till she had placed herself knee to knee with Miss Burke, and they were soon deep in calculation as to the number of " dancing gentlemen " who could be relied on for the forthcoming ball. Whether as a " dancing gentleman," or as a host, Willy could certainly be relied upon. He was now entertaining the Misses Jackson-Croly to the pitch almost of hysterics by sitting on the floor in front of them with his mouth open, while they endeavoured to throw pieces of tea-cake into it, shrieks of laughter announcing equally

the success or failure of their aim. I considerately
turned my back, and fell to a long and dull monologue
as the only method of dealing with our remaining
guest, the massive and speechless Mrs. Barrett.

A few days afterwards Mr. O'Neill rode over to ask
Willy and me to lunch at Clashmore. I had met
him and Connie once or twice out hunting. On these
occasions my acquaintance with Connie had made
rapid progress, but with her brother I seemed to have
come to a standstill. I must admit to having felt
rather disappointed at this, as since the night of the
dinner-party I had believed that, given favouring
circumstances, and a few more Corelli Suites, we
might have become reasonably good friends. On
this occasion he certainly did not carry out my
theory. After a great deal of profoundly uninteresting conversation with Willy, in which a self-respect-
ing wish not to be out of it alone induced me to make
a third, they both went round to the stables, and I
watched him ride away with a return of my old
resentment towards him.

Nevertheless, I had to allow to myself that he
had not been more dull than was suitable to the
subject on which Willy had chosen to harangue him.
The question of how and where best to lay out and
level a tennis-ground in the lawn at Durrus was not
one which lent itself to a display of epigram, but I
could not see why they should have talked about it
the whole time.

I speculated with a good deal of interest on
Nugent's probable demeanour at luncheon the next

day. I could not make up my mind if his un-
enthusiastic manner was the result of conceit or of
an inborn distrust of " Canadian young ladies." It
was certainly provoking that the one Irishman I had
hitherto met who seemed to have a few ideas beyond horses and farming was either too uninterested
or too distrustful to expend them upon me. In the
first place I was not a " Canadian young lady," and
in the second I failed to see why that should be considered a drawback.

" I suppose it is the arrogant timidity of these
eldest sons," I reflected, scornfully. " I wish I could
tell him that he can talk to me without fear of ulterior
designs on my part."

The day of the Clashmore repast was bright and
cold. Willy had put Alaska into the dog-cart to
drive me there, and we all three started very cheerfully.

" Willy," I said, as we spun along the hard road,
" you have never told me anything about The
O'Neill. I am rather nervous at the idea of meeting
an Irish chieftain in his own lair. Ought I to kiss his
hand ? I am sure you ought to have driven over
a couple of fat oxen and a he-goat as propitiatory
offerings."

" By the hokey ! I'll do nothing of the sort," said
Willy. " I can tell you, he is not the sort to refuse
them if I did ! But I've no objection to your kissing his hand, if you like."

" How kind of you ! "

" And he'll have still less. Mind you, he's a great

old buck, and expects every girl who goes to Clashmore to make love to him."

"For goodness' sake don't let him come near me!" I cried, in acute anxiety. "I never have anything to say to old men, and yet they invariably want to talk to me."

"Then, my dear, you'd better look out! The madam will have it in her sleeve for you if he's too civil ; *she* doesn't approve of his goings on."

"Well, one comfort is, I shall probably be in his black books in five minutes, as you say it is one of the seven deadly sins to call him *Mister* O'Neill. I could no more call him ' O'Neill ' than I could fly ; I should feel as if I were talking to a coachman."

"Oh, I dare say he'd put up with more than that from you ! You're just his sort. I know he'll tell every one you are ' a monstrous fine girl.' You know, he likes them tall and dark and hand——"

"Do hold your tongue ! " I interposed. "You are most offensive."

"Well, never mind," said Willy, consolingly. "May-be he won't look at you, after all. There's that big English girl we saw in church with them last Sunday—Watson, I think Nugent said her name was—I dare say he devotes himself to her all the time. Though," he added, "I don't see why I shouldn't go in for her myself "—with a glance at me to see how his shaft had sped.

"Oh, I *hope* you will ! " I said ; " it would interest me so much ! "

I thought Willy looked a little crestfallen, and he said no more on the subject.

As I walked cautiously across the highly polished floor of the Clashmore hall, preceded by an eminently respectable young footman, I was amused to find that my mind was occupied in unfeigned admiration of the cleanliness of the house. This, then, was the result of six weeks' residence at Durrus. I had become so inured to untidiness, and a generally lenient system of cleansing, that the most ordinary household virtues had acquired positive instead of merely negative value.

The big, bright drawing-room seemed full of strangers, who, as I came in, all stopped talking. I caught, however, my own name, spoken in a voice unmistakable, even in the undertone in which it said, " I declare, there's Miss Sarsfield herself ! " and I had the uncomfortable conviction that Miss Mimi Burke, in common with the rest of the room, had been discussing me.

I advanced with uncertain speed across the wide space of glowing carpet which separated me from Madam O'Neill, my last few steps being considerably accelerated by the sudden uprisal from under my feet of an abnormally lengthy dachshund, which had lain coiled unseen in my path.

" That detestable dog of Henrietta's ! " said Madam O'Neill, as she shook hands with me ; " he is always getting in the way ! How do you do, Miss Sarsfield ? Robert dear, here is Miss Sarsfield."

A stout, elderly gentleman, in a light suit of clothes,

and with one of the reddest faces I have ever seen, stepped forward with a very polite bow and expansive smile, and shook hands with me. This was my host, but the warning I had received against encouraging his attentions had so alarmed me, that as soon as was decently possible I turned my back upon him and began to talk to Henrietta. I had been aware all the time of Willy's observation, and now, as I turned and met his malevolent eye, I felt with dismay that my face was slowly turning a good fast colour, analogous to Turkey red. Deeply conscious of this, and of the unsparing glare of light from the large plate-glass windows, I spent some singularly uncomfortable moments, until the booming of the gong interrupted Miss O'Neill's comments on the weather.

I suppose that every one has at some period of life felt the absurdity of being led forth processionally to dinner, to which one is quite capable of walking unassisted on one's own legs. But to move in pomp and a tweed dress to luncheon was an unexpected ordeal. I was never more keenly alive to my own absurdity than on the present occasion, when, thrusting my hand with some difficulty inside The O'Neill's bulky arm, and feeling at least a head taller than he, we with all dignity led the way into the dining-room.

I looked round the luncheon-table to see how people had arranged themselves. My neighbour on the right was the Reverend Thomas Horan, Rector of Rathbarry, a dull-looking man, with a saffron complexion, and hair and beard of inky blackness, whose speech in private life was little less unintelligible than his pulpit utterances. Opposite to me sat Nugent O'Neill and Miss Watson. She was an ordinary type of English girl, tall, fair, fluffy-haired and well dressed, and apparently rather fond of the sound of her own high, unmodulated voice. I caught from time to time fragments of their discourse, which flowed without a check from Wagner to hockey. She, evidently, had no difficulty in talking to Nugent.

The view to my right was impeded by the portly form of Miss Mimi Burke, who was next Mr. Horan, she and that divine interchanging much lively badinage, in tones suggestive of a duet between two trombones. Beyond her I could just discern the feeble profile of Mr. Jimmy Barrett, a red-haired youth of nineteen or twenty.

The O'Neill had been up to this too busy in dissecting two ducks of unusually athletic physique to speak to me ; but he had from time to time—

> Looked upon me with a soldier's eye,
> That liked, but had a rougher task in hand.

And when the last limb had been distributed, he turned his crimson face and gleaming eyeglass upon me.

" And why haven't we seen you out with the hounds lately, Miss Sarsfield ? " he began, in a wheezy, luscious voice, with a suspicion of brogue in it. " Nugent brought home such accounts of your doings that I went out myself in hopes of seeing you show us all the way."

I modestly disclaimed all credit for the glories of the run which had made such a sensation. "And I have only been able to go out once or twice since," I added; "the meets have been so far away, and Willy has only two horses."

"Ah! I wish you'd let me give you a mount. Your grandfather has done as much for me many a day when I was a youngster; and I think you and I ought to be great friends"—this with a gaze of deep feeling from the unglazed eye.

"Thank you; you are very kind," I murmured discomposedly, looking towards the little madam to see if she were noting the behaviour of her lord.

But no; the pink ribbons and marabout tufts of her elaborate cap were nodding complacently towards Willy, who was talking to her with enviable ease and fluency.

Willy's skill in talking to elderly ladies amounted to inspiration. At present both Madam O'Neill and Miss Bessie Burke were hanging on his words, with every appearance of rapt interest; while I, the beloved of old men, could make no fitting rejoinder to the advances of my host. "But then," I reflected, in self-extenuation, "old women are infinitely preferable to old men."

"Ah yes!" The O'Neill went on, "how much you remind me of your father! The same wonderful dark eyes——"

"Mine are grey," I interrupted, in as repressive a manner as possible.

The objects in question immediately underwent a close scrutiny.

" No matter—no matter ; they have the same depth of expression. ' That eye's dark charm 'twere vain to tell,' eh ? Isn't that what Byron says ? "

Of the appropriateness of the quotation my plate alone was in a position to give an opinion, as on it my eyes were immovably fixed.

" I say, sir," said Nugent, suddenly, from across the table, " did you know that Miss Watson was a great fortune-teller ? You ought to show her your hand."

Nothing loth, O'Neill laid his fat white hand on the table for Miss Watson's inspection. She at once opened the campaign in a masterly manner, by pronouncing it to be that of a " flirt," and I felt that the chieftain's entertainment need no longer be a matter of anxiety to me.

Looking at his father with a peculiar expression, in which amusement seemed to predominate, Nugent listened for a minute or two to Miss Watson's ingenious insinuations and pronouncements. Then he turned to me.

" Do you believe in chiromancy, Miss Sarsfield ? It seems to me a useful sort of science."

CHAPTER XIV.

LUNCHEON was over. The elders of the party had returned to the drawing-room, where they were seated in a state of contented satiety, discussing their servants, their gardens, and the Church of Ireland Sustentation Fund, according to their age and kind.

In the billiard-room, a four-handed game was going on. Willy and Miss Watson were playing Connie and Mr. Barrett; and, as billiards was not one of my accomplishments, I preferred, notwithstanding polite offers of instruction, to sit in a window-seat and look on.

Nugent at first undertook the office of marker; but as he tried at the same time to explain the intricacies of the game to me, complications in the scoring soon arose, accompanied by violent altercations with the players. Finally, he was expelled with ignominy, it having been proved that he had marked Miss Watson's most brilliant break to her opponents.

" I thought I should never have come alive out of that," he said, sitting down in the window beside me; " Miss Watson looked as if she was going to convince me with the butt end of her cue, and I have no

ambition to have a row with Willy. I shouldn't
have much of a chance."

I thought, nevertheless, that he looked well able to
take care of himself, as he leaned back against the
window-shutter, and began to roll a cigarette, while
the sun slanted in upon his light, firm figure and
well-shaped head, striking a pleasant dazzle into his
blue eyes as he glanced at the players.

"Do you know Mr. Jimmy Barrett?" he asked,
in cautious tones, as that youth, his freckled face
pink with anxiety, sprawled across the table to play
his stroke.

"No, I don't know him, but I remember seeing
him out hunting."

"He can ride, that's about all he's good for. From
the look of things at present, he will have cut the
cloth to ribbons by the end of the game. If Connie
is going to give lessons in billiards, she ought to
keep a private table for her disciples."

Nugent lighted his cigarette. "Do you know,"
he continued, "I got some new fiddle music to-day.
I wonder if you could come and have a look at it?
Perhaps we could try over some?"

"I am afraid it is rather late," I said, eyeing the
players hesitatingly. "I should like it very much,
but I think the game must be nearly over, and we
ought to go home then; it gets dark so quickly."

"Oh, you've got lamps," said Nugent, getting up.
"You needn't be in such a hurry; and I know you
like playing accompaniments, you told me so yourself!"

I did remember saying so quite well, and also the manner in which the information had been received, but the idea was none the less attractive. Nugent saw the wavering in my face.

"It's really rather a decent piano," he said persuasively, "and we should have the hall to ourselves——"

It must have been quite an hour afterwards, when, with an unexplainably uneasy conscience, and a face scarlet from the mental and physical effort of reading music at sight, I obeyed Connie O'Neill's summons to tea.

In the drawing-room we found Madam O'Neill, Henrietta and Mr. Horan sitting at the tea-table, the latter with his handkerchief spread over his knees and a general greasiness of aspect suggestive of buttered toast. The Burkes had departed and, to my unbounded relief, The O'Neill did not appear. Willy and Miss Watson were standing apart from the others ; Miss Watson was holding my cousin's hand and was looking into it with a magnifying glass. He did not even look towards me, for which reason it seemed advisable that I should join them.

"Have you had your fortune told, Willy ? " I asked, with guilty solicitude.

"Yes," he said shortly. "Are you quite sure you've told me everything ? "—turning from me to Miss Watson.

"Oh dear no ! not more than half. I shall *think* about your hand, and tell you the rest another day," said Miss Watson, with great suavity. "Irishmen's hands are so puzzling—so contradictory, you know; but I suppose all Irish people are that, aren't they ? "

It was obvious that I was quite superfluous to this conversation. I retired upon tea and my hostesses, with the comfortable assurance that my cousin was in practised and capable hands.

I had but just succeeded in instructing Madam O'Neill as to my nationality, a point about which the neighbourhood was both bewildered and inquisitive, when Willy abandoned Miss Watson, and came and stood implacably before me.

" Are you nearly done your tea ? " he demanded. " The trap is at the door some time."

He remained standing before me, as if he expected me to get up at once. That he was not in the best of tempers was evident, and, feeling that delay was unadvisable, I swallowed my tea with all possible despatch, and made my adieux.

Nugent came to the hall door with us.

" Then, may I come over on Tuesday ? " he said, tucking in the rug for me, while Willy silently picked up the reins, and took the whip out of the rest, " or any other day that would suit you would do for——" The rest of the sentence was lost, as Willy, without further ceremony, drove away.

" Very well—Tuesday ! " I screamed back, as we whirled down the avenue. " My dear Willy, I don't know why you were in such a desperate hurry," I went on, rather crossly.

" Well, how was I to know he had anything more to say ? " retorted Willy, with equal ill-temper. " I'm sure he had plenty of time to settle everything before we left the house. I wasn't going to keep the mare standing, if he chose to go on prating there."

" I don't suppose another five seconds would have done her any mortal injury, and I think you might have risked it for the sake of civility."

He did not answer, and we drove along in silence, Willy maintaining a demeanour of unbending severity, and affecting to be altogether occupied with his driving.

" Very well," I said to myself, " if he likes to sulk, he may ; I won't take any notice of him."

No word was spoken for at least a mile. Alaska trotted steadily on, under the leafless beeches, and along the road by the sea, till she at length slackened to walk up a hill.

" Are you cold, Theo ? " Willy did not turn his head, but I felt that the olive branch had been extended.

" Not particularly," I said, as indifferently as possible.

" I put a wrap into the trap for you "—stretching a long arm over the back of the seat, and dragging a cloak from the depths. " You must be perished in that thin coat. Here, let me put this round you."

He wrapped me in it with unnecessary care, and while he was doing so he said suddenly :—

" I'm awfully sorry if I was rude to you. You know that——" His voice broke, and he stopped as suddenly as he had begun. I put up my hand to fasten the cloak for myself, and was rather startled to find it caught and fervently squeezed.

"Oh!" I said, withdrawing my hand sharply, "you were not in the *least* rude to me. I did not mind a bit. We had a very pleasant day on the whole, I think," I continued inconsequently ; "and did you see how beautifully I behaved to The O'Neill ? "

Willy looked a little disappointed at his apology being disposed of so quickly.

"No, I can't say I did," he answered, in an injured way. "I had plenty to do talking to the Madam."

"Yes, I saw you. I was looking at you with the deepest admiration all through lunch. And, by the way, what do you think of Miss Watson ? She seems to be a wonderful billiard-player."

"I thought you were too busy talking to Nugent to notice what we were doing," said Willy, with some return of sulkiness. "It didn't look as if you found it so hard to talk to him, as you're always saying you do."

"But I assure you we *did* look at the game, Willy. You couldn't expect me to stay and watch every stroke ! "

"Well, I only know that I spoke to you one time, and you were so much taken up with talking about music or something that you never even heard me."

"Then you must have said it absolutely in a whisper," I said, in heated self-defence. "Mr. O'Neill was not saying anything in the least interesting, only that Jimmy Barrett was cutting the cloth to ribbons, which wasn't even true."

"H'm!" said Willy, acridly, "I suppose that's why you went off with him for the whole of the afternoon. Musical flirtations are his line. I've heard many a queer story of how he carried on with a musical Yankee girl at Cannes last winter."

We rounded a turn in the road, and in the twilight I could see the Durrus woods spreading darkly down to the sea. It would take another ten minutes to reach home, and I knew that we were still on dangerous ground.

"What did Miss Watson say of your hand?" I asked, with the view of changing the conversation. "Did she tell you that you had 'no sense of humour, and homicidal tendencies combined with unusual conscientiousness?' That's what a man once told me."

"No," answered Willy, rising to the fly sulkily, "she didn't say very much about my character. She was looking at my line of heart most of the time, I think. She told me that I would have 'two great passions' in my life, and that I was to be married soon." He stopped, and looked at me.

"How exciting!" I said hurriedly. "My man did not tell me any of those interesting sort of things."

"She said my line of fate was broken," resumed Willy, "whatever that may mean. She told me I had a very good line of intellect, but it wasn't properly developed. I dare say the last part of that's true enough," he added, with a sigh. "I never got a chance to learn anything when I was a boy; if my mother had lived it would have been different. The governor sent me from one dirty little school to another for a couple or three years, and then the National School master had a go at me, and that's about all the education I ever had."

"I dare say you get on just as well without being very good at classics and those sort of things. And, you see, you passed your exam. for your captaincy in the West Cork quite easily," I said, with a lame attempt at consolation.

"That's quite a different thing; any fool could do that. What makes me sick is to see Nugent and chaps like him, who have been to Harrow and Oxford and all the rest of it—and here I've been stuck all my life, without a chance to get level with them. It's when I'm talking to you that I feel what an ignorant brute I am!"

"I hate to hear you talk like that," I said, hurt by the pain in his voice. "*I* never thought you so —not for an instant. On the contrary, I think you know more than any one I ever met—about practical things; and if you don't look where you're going, you will drive over old Moll—" as we turned sharply off the road at the Durrus lodge.

"A good job too!" said Willy, roughly, "—teach her to keep out of the way!"

CHAPTER XV.

It was early in December, a showery, blustery afternoon; but I was sitting out of doors in the hay. The men had been cutting away the great rick in the haggard; they had taken a slice off it, down almost to the ground, and I had burrowed myself a comfortable bed among the soft trusses, with my back against the bristling, newly shorn wall of hay that towered above me like a gable. The dogs were standing beside in different attitudes of intensest attention, their eyes fixed, like mine, upon a hole in the foundations of the rick, from which at this moment a pair of legs in corduroys and gaiters were protruding.

"Have you come to them yet?" I called out.

A muffled grunt was all that I could hear in answer; but after a moment or two, the body belonging to the legs was drawn out of the hole.

"I've got one of the brutes," said Willy, holding up his hand, with a ferret hanging limply from it. "I don't know how I'll get the other; those rats must be miles back in the rick. I'll have to go up for one of the young Sweenys to help me to move some of the stones under the rick."

"I think in that case I shall go home," I said.
"I suppose you'll take hours over it."

"Oh no! Do wait a bit; we won't be any time.
You can have my coat if you're cold," said Willy,
dropping the reclaimed ferret into its bag. "I'll be
back in half a minute."

He climbed the wall of the haggard, and took a
short cut across the field to where the whitewashed
walls of Sweeny's cottage showed through the twigs
of the leafless fuchsia hedge that incongruously surrounded it and its manure heaps and pig-sties.

I took out my watch as soon as he had started, and
saw that it was half-past three. Willy seemed to
have forgotten that this Tuesday afternoon was the
one on which Nugent had said he would come over.
I had taken care to say something about it at breakfast, but had done it so lamely and inopportunely
that I was not sure whether Willy had heard me;
and moral cowardice had prevented me from re-
minding him of it when he had asked me after
luncheon to come out with him to the haggard,
where a thriving colony of rats had been that
morning discovered.

Willy and I were now on terms of the most absolute intimacy. His daily companionship had become
second nature to me—something which I accepted as
a matter of course, which gave me no trouble, and
was in all ways pleasant. But, for all that, I had
begun to find out that in some occult way I was a
little afraid of him. He was unexpectedly and
minutely observant, and, where I was concerned,

light, I had at first noticed. In the smoky shadow of the overhanging chimney-place was huddled, on a three-legged stool, a very small old man in knee-breeches and a tail-coat, who was smoking a short pipe, and still held in his hand the battered tall hat which he had taken off on our entrance. He was our hostess's father-in-law, one of the oldest tenants on the estate, and he sat, as I had often seen the old countrymen in the cabins sit, smoking and dozing over the fire, and looking hardly more alive to what was going on than the grey, smouldering lumps of turf on the hearth. In the dusky recess at the foot of a four-poster bed, which blocked up one of the small windows, Batty and two other children were hiding behind each other, and were staring at us as young birds might. Pat and Jinny were vulgarly snuffing among Mrs. Sweeny's pots and pans, with an affectation of starvation which but ill-assorted with what I knew of their recent luncheon. Now they had come, with stunning unexpectedness, on a cat, crouched on the dresser, and, when called off by Willy on the very eve of battle, remained for the rest of their visit shaken by paroxysms of shuddering, in agonised contemplation of her security. From a hencoop in the corner by the bed came faint cluckings ; the goose which Mrs. Sweeny had been plucking lay with its legs tied beside the red earthen pan, in which it might have seen its own breast feathers, and tried to console itself by pecking feebly at the yellow meal which had been spilt on the ground in front of the chicken's coop.

5

Mrs. Sweeny was sitting on a kind of rough settle, between the other window and the door of an inner room. She was a stout, comfortable-looking woman of about forty, with red hair and quick blue eyes, that roved round the cabin, and silenced with a glance the occasional whisperings that rose from the children.

" And how's the one that had the bad cough ? " asked Willy, pursuing his conversation with her with his invariable ease and dexterity. " Honor her name is, isn't it ? "

" See, now, how well he remembers ! " replied Mrs. Sweeny. " Indeed, she's there back in the room, lyin' these three days. Faith, I think 'tis like the decline she have, Masther Willy."

" Did you get the doctor to her ? " said Willy. " I'll give you a ticket if you haven't one."

" Oh, indeed, Docthor Kelly's afther givin' her a bottle, but sure, I wouldn't let her put it into her mouth at all. God knows what'd be in it. Wasn't I afther throwin' a taste of it on the fire to thry what'd it do, and Phitz ! says it, and up with it up the chimbley ! Faith, I'd be in dread to give it to the child. Sure, if it done that in the fire, what'd it do in her inside ? "

" Well, you're a greater fool than I thought you were," said Willy, politely.

" May-be I am, faith," replied Mrs. Sweeny, with a loud laugh of enjoyment. " But if she's for dyin', the crayture, she'll die aisier without thim thrash of medicines ; and if she's for livin', 'tisn't thrusting to them she'll be. Sure, God is good—God is good——"

"Divil a betther!" interjected old Sweeny, un-expectedly.

It was the first time he had spoken, and having delivered himself of this trenchant observation, he relapsed into silence and the smackings at his pipe.

"Don't mind him at all, your honour, miss," said his daughter-in-law, to me. "Sure, he's only a silly owld man."

"He's a good deal more sensible than you are," said Willy, returning to the subject of Honor.

The rain poured steadily down. I thought of Nugent, and could fancy his surprise at hearing that I was not at home. It was not, I argued to myself, so much that I was sorry to miss him, as that I hated being rude; and it certainly was rude to have gone out on the day he had settled to come, without even leaving a message. What an amazing gift of the gab Willy had! Rain or no rain, it was clear that he and Mrs. Sweeny meant to talk to one another for the rest of the afternoon.

The old man in the chimney-corner had watched me during all this time, and muttered to himself every now and then—what, I could not understand. We must have been sitting there for ten minutes at least, when the two boys whom Willy had left to look for the ferret came dripping in, with the object of their search safely housed in a bag, and silently stationed themselves along with their brothers and sisters in the corner by the bed.

"Is the rain nearly over?" I asked the elder.

"I dunno, miss," he replied, bashfully rubbing

the sole of his foot up and down the shin of the other leg.

" I can tell you that," said Willy, getting up and going to the door. " I don't think it looks like clearing for another quarter of an hour."

" Then I don't know what I can do," I said, in unguarded consternation.

" Why," said Willy, turning round and looking at me with his hands in his pockets, "what's the hurry ? "

" There is no hurry exactly," I said, feeling very small and cowardly ; " but I thought you knew—at least, I think I told you this morning, that Mr. O'Neill said he would come over to-day."

I wondered if this simple sentence gave any indication of the effort it was to me to say it.

" I can't say I remember anything about it," Willy answered, in what I am sure he thought a crushingly chilly voice.

" Oh yes, indeed I did tell you," I said, getting up and following him to the door ; "but you sneezed just as I was saying it, and the voice is not yet created that could be heard through one of your sneezes."

I knew that he was rather proud than otherwise of his noisy sneezes, and I laughed servilely, and looked up, hoping that he would laugh too. But there was nothing approaching to amusement in his face. It was red and forbidding, as he looked out into the rain that was thrashing down in the dirty yard. He had still a good deal of hay and hayseed about his

CHAPTER XVI.

The rain was not by any means over when we came out into the field. It was half-past four, but, though the sun had sunk, the clouds had lifted, and the misty orange light of the after-glow filled the air. A slim scrap of a moon had slipped up over the hill to the eastward, and the bats were swooping round our heads as we picked our way across the muddy yard of the demesne farm.

"I think you'll find the field drier than the bohireen," said Willy, in the same distant voice with which he had last spoken; "we can get over the wall here."

He took my hand to help me over, but dropped it as quickly as possible, and walked on with unnecessary haste, keeping a little in front of me. The field was, as he had said, rather better than the lane, but my feet sank in the soaked ground, the pace at which we were going took my breath away, and I began to be left behind. Willy still stalked on unrelentingly, with the enviable unpetticoated ease of mankind in wet weather.

"I wish you wouldn't go so fast," I called out at last. "I can't possibly keep up if you go at that pace."

He slackened at once.

" I thought you wanted to go fast," he answered, without looking back.

" I don't particularly care," I said, as I struggled up alongside of him. " I should think Mr. O'Neill must have gone home some time ago."

Willy made no comment. I took out my handkerchief and wiped the last raindrops from my face, feeling a good deal aggrieved by his behaviour.

" Your cap's all wet too," he said, looking down at me from under his eyelids—" soaking, and so is your coat," putting his hand on my shoulder for a moment. " I think I ought to have carried you home in a turf-basket. Look at this bad bit here we've got to go through."

" Thank you," I said snappishly, taking off my wet cap and shaking the rain from it as I went, " I should rather not. I am about as wet as I can be now. It certainly was capital weather to go out ferreting in."

We were now at the " bad bit," of which Willy had spoken,—a broad, dark stripe, vivid green by daylight,—across a hollow in the field, with a gleam of water here and there in it.

" You'd much better let me carry you over this," said Willy, stopping.

" No, thank you," I said again, eyeing, however, with an inward tremor, the long distances between the tussocks of grass which might serve as stepping-stones. " You have the eggs to carry, and I have no wish to be dropped with them into the bog."

" Ah ! nonsense now ; you know there's no fear of

that," he said, and put his arm round me as if to lift me. " Do let me."

" I am *not* going to be carried," I said, with determination. " If you'd only let me alone, I should get over quite well."

He did not take his arm away, and bent down over me.

" You're always getting angry with me these times," he said.

" No, indeed I'm not," I answered, trying to speak pleasantly, and to move forward at the same time.

His quick breathing was at my ear, and for one moment his lips touched my hair ; the next I was floundering with a burning face through the deepest of the quagmire. At every step my feet sank ankle-deep ; I dragged out each in succession with an effort that nearly pulled my boots off, and when I gained firm ground again, my feet had become shapeless brown objects, weighed down with mud, with which my skirt was also thickly coated. Willy had made no further effort to help me, and, having followed me across with caution, walked silently beside me as I hurried along, trying to ignore my uncomfortable and ignoble plight.

But one field now divided us from the road, and as I scrambled up on to the high fence I heard wheels, and saw something moving along it away from the Durrus gate.

" That must be Mr. O'Neill's trap ! " I cried excitedly, jumping down after Willy, who was already

in the field. " Oh, Willy, do run and stop him ! I
must explain——"

" There's no earthly use in trying to catch him
now," Willy answered morosely. " I'm not going to
kill myself running after him, like a fool, for nothing
at all."

" Very well," I rejoined ; " if you won't go, I will."

My indignation with Willy alone sustained me
through that dreadful run. I had to cut diagonally
across the field in order to intercept Nugent. The
ground was soft and sticky ; my mud-encumbered
skirt clung round me ; and I should have had scant
chance of catching him but for the fact that the road,
curving a little at this point, led over a steep and
stony bit of hill. I reached the wall of the field just
as the horse was breaking into a trot at the top of the
hill ; but, fortunately for me, the groom at the back
of the dog-cart saw the walking-stick which I feebly
brandished to attract his attention—I had no breath
wherewith to shout—and, recognising me, called to
his master to stop.

Nugent pulled up, and, turning round, took off his
hat with a face of such astonishment that I became
all at once aware of the appearance which I must
present, but I came forward with a gallant attempt
to appear unconscious of my heated face and general
dishevelledness.

" How are you ? " I panted. " I intended to be at
home. Won't you——? " Here my breath failed
me, and I was obliged to eke out my sentence with
a gesture in the direction of Durrus.

"Oh, thanks; it doesn't matter in the least. Don't let me take you back any sooner than you had intended," replied Nugent, in a voice that told he had been nursing his wrath to keep it warm.

"I was going home," I said, more intelligibly. "I am very sorry, but we were delayed by the rain."

He got out of the dog-cart and shook hands with me across the low wall, on the farther side of which I was standing.

"There has certainly been a pretty heavy shower," he said, looking at me uncertainly, but, as I thought, with a dawning amusement.

"Hasn't there? Awful!" I said, smearing my wet hair back behind my ears, and putting on the cap which I had clutched convulsively in my hand during my run across the field. "We had to shelter in a cottage for ever so long."

"Who are we?"

I looked round for my late companion, but he was nowhere to be seen.

"Willy was with me," I said; "but he declared that it was no use trying to catch you, and—and I suppose he has gone home."

Nugent said nothing, but climbed on to the wall with as much dignity as his mackintosh would permit, and helped me over it. I was very unfortunate, I inwardly reflected; I first got wet through, and then one cross young man after another dragged me over these horrible wet stone walls. However, I said aloud—

"You must come back and have some tea; it is quite early still."

He hesitated.

"Thanks, I am not sure if I shall have time; but perhaps, in any case, you had better let me drive you home."

The step of the dog-cart was a very high one, and as I put my foot on it to get up, the full beauties and proportions of my boot—a shapeless mass, resembling a brown paper parcel—were revealed. My eyes met Nugent's, and we both laughed, he unwillingly, I with hopeless realisation of my appearance.

"I am not fit to get into anything better than a pig-sty or a donkey-cart," I said apologetically. "I really am ashamed of myself from every point of view, moral and physical."

"But what on earth have you been doing?" he asked, as we turned and drove towards Durrus. "Have you been out snipe-shooting in the bog with Willy?"

"No," I answered cheerfully; "something much more vulgar."

"It certainly does look more as if you and he had been digging potatoes, but I did not quite like to suggest that."

Something in his manner offended me.

"That was just it," I said, not choosing to explain. "Willy is rather short of farm hands just now, and I have had my first lesson in 'sticking' potatoes."

"I should have thought 'sticking' horse-dealers was more in Willy's line!"

"I mean to learn that as well," I said combatively. "Probably the next time you see me, I shall be selling pigs in the fair at Esker!"

"Very likely. I believe Americans—I beg your pardon, I mean people from Canada—like to do a country thoroughly when they get there. I suppose you go in for experiments as much as the others?"

"Why, certainly! I'm experimentalising all the time."

"Really!" said Nugent, without appearing to notice my elaborate Americanisms. "And is your experiment successful so far?" He looked me full in the face as he spoke.

"Yes, so far," I answered, with an unexplainable feeling that sincerity was required of me, and noting inwardly the blue impenetrability of his eyes.

He said nothing for a minute or two; then, without any apparent connection of ideas—

"Is Willy coming home to hear us play?" he asked. "Have you taught him to appreciate high-class music yet?"

"I don't think he wants any teaching," I said, with an instinctive wish to stand up for my cousin; "he has a wonderful ear, and his taste is really very good."

"Really!"

The manner was unimpeachable, but there was challenge in the voice.

"Yes," I said positively; "I believe he has a real talent for music, if he had only been given a chance."

" He did not get much of a chance at anything, I believe," Nugent said, in what seemed to me a patronising way.

" No, he certainly did not. I think very few people know all the disadvantages he has had, and I am quite sure that very few people would have done as well as he has if they had been in his place." This with some warmth.

" I am sure I shouldn't, for one," replied Nugent, quietly taking to himself the generality which I had thought both telling and impalpable. " But then, I dare say——Why, there he is ! " interrupting himself, as we turned into the avenue and came in sight of Willy, who was walking very fast towards home.

He got out of our way without looking back, and only nodded to us as we passed. I saw the bowl of eggs in his hand, and knew by the defiant way in which he carried it that he was ashamed of it.

" Your fellow-labourer seems to have had a peaceful time in the hen-house whilst you were sticking the potatoes," said Nugent, with again the suggestion of a sneer. " He certainly does not look as if he had done as much hard work as you."

" No ; he has not run all the way across a field, as I did just now."

Nugent coloured. " I deserved that," he said, and laughed. Then, after a moment's pause, " And I don't think I did deserve your taking such trouble to stop me."

" Of course, you may have some inner sense of unworthiness," I answered, mollified, " that must remain between you and your own conscience; but it was very rude of me not to have been at home, and I did not mind the run half so much as writing the letter of apology which I should have felt you had a right to."

"And which I should not have believed," said Nugent. "It was so wet that I should have been quite certain that you were sitting over the fire with Willy all the time, and told Roche to send me away because you felt as if playing violin accompaniments would be a bore."

"Appearances would have been against me," I admitted; "but I should have enclosed my boots as circumstantial evidence"—advancing one disreputable foot from beneath the rug—"and perhaps also one of the potato cakes that I had ordered specially for your benefit."

A loud twanging snap from the violin-case under the seat startled us both.

"By Jove!" exclaimed Nugent, "that is the E string, and I have not another with me."

"Then we can't have any music," I said, with unaffected dismay. "What a pity! So I brought you back for nothing, after all."

"Don't say nothing," he said; "think of the potato cakes!"

"That may be your point of view," I said regretfully; "but when I was running across that field I was thinking of Corelli."

"I had hoped," remarked Nugent, looking sideways at me, as he pulled up at the hall door, "that you might have had some incidental thoughts about the way in which you had treated me."

"I cannot argue any more until I have had my tea," I said, getting out of the trap, and trying to stamp some of the mud off my boots on the steps.

"Perhaps I had better go home," he suggested. "As Corelli is out of the question, I suppose I shall not be wanted."

"Just as you like."

"But I want the potato cake you promised me."

"Then, I think you had better come in and get it," I said, going into the house; "I don't approve of outdoor relief!"

CHAPTER XVII.

NOVEMBER 20th was Willy's twenty-fifth birthday, and he and I fitly celebrated it by going out hunting, and, having come home hungry after a good day's sport, were now, in consideration of having had no lunch, indulging in poached eggs at afternoon tea.

" The men in the yard tell me that there are to be great doings to-night in honour of me," Willy remarked, when the first sharp edge had been taken off his appetite. " There's to be a bonfire outside the front gate, and Conneen the piper, and dancing, and everything. It means that I'll have to send them a tierce of porter, and that you'll have to turn out after dinner and go down and have a look at them."

" So long as they don't ask me to dance, I shall be very glad to go. But would your father mind ? "

" Mind ? Not he ! You're such a ' white-headed boy ' with him, you can do what you like with him. By Jove, he's a deal fonder of you than he ever was of me ! " said Willy, with ungrudging admiration.

" I am sure he is not," I said lazily, and as much for the sake of contradiction as from any false modesty. " It is most unlikely. I know if I were he, I should naturally like you better than I like myself."

"What on earth are you trying to say?" said Willy. "Would you mind saying it all over again— slowly?"

"I mean," I said, slightly confused, but sticking to my point—"I mean that if I were your father, I should see a great many more reasons for being fond of *you* than I should of *me*."

"Well, as far as I can make that out," said Willy, grinning exasperatingly, "it seems to me that it's a pity you're not my father."

"You know perfectly well what I mean. Just suppose that I was your father——"

"I'd rather not, thanks."

I did not heed the interruption. "I should be much fonder of you——"

"Then, why aren't you?"

"I don't care what you say," I said, feeling I was getting the worst of it; "I know what I mean quite well, and so would you, only that you choose to be an idiot." And, getting up, I left the room with all speed, in order to have the last word in a discussion which was taking a rather difficult tone.

The sea-fog had crept up from the harbour towards evening, and it fell in heavy drops from the trees upon Willy and me as we walked down the avenue after dinner to see the bonfire. There was no moon visible, but the milky atmosphere held some luminous suggestion of past or coming light. It was a still night; we could hear the low booming of the sea in the caves below the old graveyard, and the nearer splashing of the rising tide among the Durrus rocks.

"There's no sound I hate like that row the ground-swell makes out there at the point," said Willy. "If you're feeling any way lonely, it makes you want to hang yourself."

"I like it," I said, stopping to listen. "I often lie awake and listen to it these nights, when the westerly wind is blowing."

"May-be you'd get enough of doing that if you were here by yourself for a bit, and knew you'd got to stop here. I tell you you've no notion what this place is like in the winter. Sometimes there's not a creature in the country to speak to from one month's end to another."

"I ought to know something about it by this time."

"You think you do," he answered, with a short laugh. "But you can't very well know what it was like before you came, no more than you can tell what it will be like when you're gone."

We moved on again.

"Cannot you ever get away?" I asked sympathetically.

"No; how could I leave the governor? I tell you," he went on, "that if you were boxed up here with no one to talk to but him, you'd go anywhere for company." He stopped for a moment. "Do you know that, before you came here last October, I was as near making a fool of myself as ever a chap was"—breaking off again, but continuing before I could speak—" I believe I didn't care a hang what I did with myself then. I suppose you'll think that I'm an ass, but it's very hard to have no one at all who cares about you."

" I am sure it must be," I said, feeling rather uncomfortable, and walking quickly on. Confidences of this kind from Willy were quite new. They were also embarrassing, and the friendly and cousinly footing that I thought we had arrived at seemed more precarious than it had been.

We were now near the gate, and could already hear the squeals of the bagpipes, and see the glare of the bonfire in the fog. All round the semicircular sweep outside the lodge, a row of women and girls were seated on the ground, with their backs to the ivy-covered wall, while a number of men and boys were heaping sticks on to a great glowing mound of turf that was burning in the middle of the road. The barrel of porter which Willy had sent was propped up in one of the niches in the wall, and in the other niches, and along the top of the walls, were clustered innumerable little boys.

As Willy and I came through the open gates, a sort of straggling cheer was set up by the men, which was shrilly augmented and prolonged by shrieks from the children in the niches. Willy walked up to the bonfire.

" Well, boys," he said, " that's a great bonfire you have. I'm glad to see you all here."

At this moderate display of eloquence there was another cheer, and as it died away, a very old man, in knee-breeches and tail-coat, came forward, and, to my intense amazement, kissed Willy's hand.

" I'm a tenant in Durrus eighty-seven years," he said, " an' if I was dyin' this minute, I'd say you were the root and branch of your grandfather's family ! Root and branch—root and branch ! "

Here his eloquence was cut short by an old woman, who darted forward and snatched Willy's hand from the man. She also began by kissing it resoundingly, but, in a transport of adoration, she flung it from her.

" On the mout' ! on the mout' ! " she screamed, flinging her arms round him ; then, dragging his face down to hers, she suited the action to the word.

Willy submitted with admirable fortitude ; but, in order to avoid further demonstrations of a similar kind, he called upon Conneen the piper to play a jig. I heard from the other side of the road a long preliminary drone, and the piper, a crippled hunchback, with long black hair and a sallow face, seated on a donkey, began to produce from his bagpipes a succession of grunts and squeals of varying discordancy, known as " The Foxhunter's Jig."

I drew back into the smaller gateway to watch the dance. The figures of the four dancers showed darkly against the background of firelit, steamy fog, and the flames of a tar-barrel which had just been thrown upon the bonfire glared unsteadily on the faces of the people, and on the glowing network of branches overhead. Willy was one of the four who were dancing, and was covering himself with glory by the number and intricacy of his steps. He had chosen as his partner the buxom Mrs. Sweeny, in whose cottage we had once sheltered from the rain, and above the piercing efforts of the bagpipes to render in "The Foxhunter's Jig" the various noises of the chase, the horn, the hounds, and the hunters, the plaudits of the audience rose with more and more enthusiasm.

"More power, Masther Willy!"

"Tighten yourself now, Mrs. Sweeny!"

"God knows Mrs. Sweeny's a lovely dancer! She'd dance on a plate!"

"Ah ha! d'ye mind that for a lep! He's the divil's own dancer!"

I looked on and listened to it all from the gateway, feeling, in spite of my Sarsfield blood, a stranger in a strange land. I did not recognise many of the people about me; beyond some of the junior members of the Durrus household, who nodded to me with the chastened, reserved friendliness of the domestic servant when away from her own roof, and Bridget Courtney, the washerwoman, whose white teeth shone in a broad grin when I looked at her, I knew no one. Neither Anstey nor her mother were anywhere to be seen, though I had looked up and down the row of faces several times for them. A grizzled, bearded man, whom I knew to be Michael Brian, the lodge-keeper, was in charge of the barrel of porter. I noticed during the dance that, although he never took his eyes off the dancers, he did not applaud, and before it was over he left the barrel in the care of a subordinate, and went past me into the lodge.

In a minute or two he returned, bringing Anstey with him, and she began to help him in dispensing the porter. The niche in which it was placed was quite near to where I was standing, and I could hear him scolding her in a low voice. She looked frightened and unhappy : I thought with a kind of horror of the dumb and distraught mother, alone in the darkened lodge.

When the jig had ended with a long squeal from the pipes, intended, I presumed, to represent the fox's death-agony, Willy led his breathless partner back to her place, and slowly made his way to me, amid a shower of compliments and pious ejaculations.

" Phew ! I'm mostly dead ! " he said, leaning against the gatepost beside me, and fanning himself with his cap. " Mrs. Sweeny has more going in her than ten men, and dancing on the gravel is no joke."

While he was speaking, I saw that his eye had fallen on Anstey, and almost imperceptibly he faced more and more in my direction, till his back was turned to her and her father. Another dance began, but, instead of joining in it, he lighted a cigarette and went on talking to me.

" Perhaps we'd better be getting home," he said presently. " You must have seen about enough of it."

We moved from where we were standing into the carriage-drive, and he said a general good-night to the assemblage. The jig was stopped, and one of the dancers shouted—

" Three cheers for Masther Willy ! "

" Huzzay ! " rose the chorus.

" And three cheers for Miss Sarsfield ! " called out another voice, which, with deep gratification, I recognised as that of Mrs. Rourke, the Durrus cook, and another " Huzzay ! " arose in my honour.

Willy looked at me with a beaming face.

" Do you hear that, Theo ? You see, *they* think a good deal of you too."

" It's very kind of them," I replied, retreating precipitately into the darkness ; " but I hope they don't expect me to make a speech."

" Masther Willy ! "

I heard a hoarse whisper behind me, and, looking back, I saw that Michael Brian had followed Willy through the gates.

" Masther Willy, aren't you goin' to dance with my gerr'l ? "

" No, I'm not : I'm going home," said Willy, roughly. He turned away, but Brian caught his sleeve.

" Ah ! come back now and dance with her," he said, in a part bullying, part wheedling voice ; " don't give her the go-by."

Willy wrenched away his sleeve.

" Go to the devil ! You're drunk ! " he said, in a low angry voice.

" Dhrunk is it ? Wait a while, and you'll see if I'm dhrunk," said Brian, following him as he turned from him, and speaking more threateningly. " Dhrunk or sober, there'll be work yet before ye're done with me."

Willy made no remark on what had taken place as he joined me where I was standing a few paces in advance of him. I did not know what to say, and we walked silently away up the avenue. The noise of the bagpipes died away behind us in the fog, and the moaning rush of the tide, now full in, on the strand, was again the only sound to be heard. We had got into the darkness of the clump of elms, when Willy stopped short.

" I thought I heard some one there in the trees," he said. " I wonder if that blackguard——" He did not finish the sentence, and we both listened.

" I don't hear anything now, whatever," he said, moving on. But before we had gone more than a few steps, I heard a twig snap.

" There *is* something there," I said apprehensively, coming closer to him. He felt for my hand, and put it into his arm.

" Never mind ; very likely it's only a stray jackass ; don't be frightened at all."

We walked on quickly until we were in the open beyond the little wood, and we were near the house before he spoke again.

" Theo, I think I've made the most miserable hash of my life that ever any one did. Why didn't you come here long ago ? " he broke off, and laid his hand on mine that was resting on his arm. " You needn't think I'm going to bother you about my-self—but I just feel that everything's gone against me."

" Oh, that's nonsense, Willy ! " I said, trying to

speak with more cheerfulness than I felt. " That is a very poor way of looking at things."

" Very likely, but it's the only way I've got." We were on the steps by this time, and he opened the hall door. " Anyhow, it doesn't make much difference how I look at them ; I suppose it will all come to the same sooner or later."

He shut the door with a bang, and I went upstairs.

CHAPTER XVIII.

It was the day of the Jackson-Crolys' dance, for which we had in due course received our invitations, gorgeously printed on gilt-edged cards. Willy and I were sitting over the library fire after tea, and had already begun to contemplate the combined horrors of dressing for a ball and eating a half-past six o'clock dinner, when Uncle Dominick stalked in, with a basket in his hand, which he handed to me with a note, saying austerely that one of the Clashmore servants had just ridden over with it.

The note was from Connie.

" My dear Theo," it began—I had seen a good deal of the O'Neills lately, and Connie and I had arrived at calling each other by our Christian names —" we are sending you over some yellow chrysanthemums, as you said you were going to wear white. Mamma will, of course, be delighted to chaperon you, and thinks you had better come here first, and drive on in our carriage ; and we can take you home and put you up for the night, as Willy may want to stay later than you do. Nugent is very proud of the bouquet. He constructed it himself, and has spent the greater part of the morning over it in the conservatory. Certainly, as far as wire goes, it is all that can be desired ; there are at least ten yards in it."

" I should have thought you might have found some flowers for your cousin here, Willy," remarked Uncle Dominick, while I was reading the letter.

" There's nothing fit for any one to wear," answered Willy, gloomily. " I was out this morning to see, and there was nothing but a few violets."

" I am sorry you did not pick them," I said, with pacific intention ; " I should have been very glad to wear them. They think it would simplify matters if I slept at Clashmore to-night," I went on. " I think it would be a good plan, if you don't mind, Uncle Dominick ? "

" It is entirely for you to decide, my dear," he said coldly ; " you can make any arrangements that you like. The man is waiting for an answer."

" Well, I *will* sleep there," I said, goaded to decision by his ungracious manner.

With the aid of the ministrations of Maggie, the red-haired housemaid, who had developed a deep attachment for me, I was arriving at the more advanced stages of my toilet, when I heard a knock at my door.

" I've got you some violets," said Willy's voice, " but I'm afraid they're not up to much. I've left them outside."

I heard him run down the passage to his own room, and, opening the door, I saw a small bunch of violets lying on the ground. I picked them up; there were very few of them, and they were drenched with rain. Willy must have been all this time toilsomely searching for them with a lantern in the dark.

" Has it been raining, Maggie ? " I asked.

" 'Deed, then, it has, miss, and teeming rain this half-hour."

So he must have gone out in the rain to pick them for me. Poor Willy !

I fastened them into the front of my dress with an ache of pity, and looked at those other flowers on my dressing-table, the feathery golden chrysanthemums showing through a mist of maiden-hair, with something that was near being distaste. Their coming had not been altogether a surprise to me : in fact, I had been more or less looking out for them all day. But somehow Willy's bunch of violets had taken away most of my pleasure in them, and when I came downstairs I laid the bouquet with my wraps out of sight, on the hall table.

We hurried through our early dinner, but before we left the dining-room I received a mysterious intimation from Roche to the effect that Mrs. Rourke would like to see me outside.

Mrs. Rourke was the cook, and, inly marvelling what she could have to say to me, I went out into the hall. There, to my no small surprise, I was confronted, not only by Mrs. Rourke, but by the whole strength of the Durrus indoor establishment. There they all were—housemaid, dairymaid and kitchen-maid, with their barefooted subordinates lurking behind them, and from them, as I appeared, a low-breathed murmur of approval arose.

"Well, miss," began Mrs. Rourke, in tones of solemn conviction, "ye might thravel Ireland this night, and ye wouldn't find yer aiqual! Of all the young ladies ever I seen, you take the sway!"

"Glory be to God! 'tis thrue!" moaned the kitchenmaid, in awestricken assent.

"Why, you can't half see her there, Mrs. Rourke," said Willy, coming out of the dining-room; "hold on till I get a lamp."

He came back with the tall old moderator lamp from the middle of the dinner-table, and, holding it up, stood so that the light should fall full on me. Seldom have I felt more foolish than I did at that moment; but I did my best to live up to the position.

"And what I say, Masther Willy," continued Mrs. Rourke, taking up her parable in the manner of a prophetess, "is that I never seen a finer pair than the two of ye, and ye do well to be proud of her! And I hope it won't be the last time I'll see herself and yourself going out through that door together—nor coming in through it nayther!"

This dark saying was received by the chorus with various devotional expressions of satisfaction.

"Yes, Mrs. Rourke," said my uncle's voice from behind me, in tones of unusual affability, "I think we have no reason to be ashamed of our representatives."

I was beginning to feel that I could bear this dreadful ceremonial no longer, when, with sincere inward thanksgiving, I heard the grinding of wheels on the gravel.

"There's the carriage," I said, turning to Willy, who had all this time been silently holding up the lamp; "do put down that thing, and get me my cloak."

My uncle himself put my wraps upon me, and stood with me in the open doorway, while Roche laid a strip of carpet down the wet steps. As I stood waiting in the doorway, I saw a woman standing in the rain, just outside the circle of light thrown from the carriage lamps. She pressed forward as I came down the steps, and then drew quickly back with what sounded like a sob. The momentary gleam of the carriage lights had shown me who it was.

"Willy," I said, as we drove away, "did you see Anstey Brian standing there? I am almost sure she was crying. What could have been the matter with her?"

"You must have made a mistake," he said; "may-be it wasn't Anstey at all. Anyhow, if she wants to cry, there's no need for her to go and stand out there in the rain to do it."

He spoke with an impatience that puzzled me. I was quite certain that I had seen Anstey; but, remembering that for some reason the subject of Moll Hourihane and her daughter had always been an unfortunate one with Willy and my uncle, I said no more.

We had been asked to the Jackson-Crolys' for nine o'clock, but, although it was not much more than

half-past when the Clashmore carriage arrived at
Mount Prospect, several heated couples whom we
encountered in the hall were proof that the dancing
had already been going on for some time. On coming down from the cloak-room, we saw at the foot
of the stairs a small, bald-headed gentleman, moving
in an agitated way from leg to leg, and apparently
engaged in alternately putting on and taking off his
gloves.

"That's Mr. Jackson-Croly," whispered Connie,
rapidly ; " he's an *odious* little thing ! Don't dance
with him if you can possibly help it. I always tell
lies to escape him ; I lose less self-respect in that
way than by dancing with him."

She had no time to say more, as Madam O'Neill
had by this time advanced upon our host with a
benignity of aspect born of the consciousness of a
singularly becoming cap and generally successful
toilette. For a moment I thought he was going to
make her a courtesy, so low was his reverence on
shaking hands with her.

"It was *so* kind of you to come, Madam O'Neill,"
he said, speaking through tightly closed teeth in
a small, deprecating voice ; " and the weather so
unpleasant, too ; yes, indeed ! But we've quite a
nice little number of friends dancing in there
already, and we're expecting another carful of
partners for the young ladies"—with a bow to
Connie and me—"from Doctor Foley's Seminary
in Esker."

"That will be delightful ! " said Connie, with a

brilliant smile, giving me at the same time an expressive pinch.

She was looking very pretty, and was in the highest spirits, consequent, as I soon found, on an advanced flirtation with a Captain Forster, then staying at Clashmore. Pending his arrival, however, she condescended to dance with Mr. Jimmy Barrett, who, his usual red-hot appearance accentuated by the fact that he was wearing the hunt coat, had waylaid us in the hall, and he now carried Connie off, while I followed the Madam and Mr. Jackson-Croly into the drawing-room. There we were received by Mrs. Jackson-Croly, imposingly attired in ruby silk and white lace. Unlike her obsequious spouse, Madam O'Neill's diamonds and acknowledged social standing had no overawing effect upon her, and in her greeting to us she abated no whit of her usual magnificence of manner.

" 'Twas too bad Miss O'Neill was from home and couldn't come," she observed condescendingly. " I have lots of gentlemen looking for partners—quite an *embarras de richesses*. There were so many asking for invitations, and I didn't like refusing. You must let me present some of them to you, Miss Sarsfield."

The two rooms in which the dancing was going on were brightened by the red coats of several members of the Esker Hunt, and one of these was presently captured by Mrs. Croly and introduced to me. While I was putting his name down for a dance, the rest of our party were ushered in by Mr. Jackson-Croly.

" The Clashmore gentlemen, Louisa, my dear," he announced, with chastened pride.

The O'Neill soon made his way to me.

" Well, Miss Sarsfield, what are we to have ? I see the next is a polka. I can't manage these new-fashioned waltzes, but I flatter myself I *can* dance a polka."

With inward trepidation I consented, and was occupied with the usual difficulty of refastening my pencil to my card, when card and all were quietly taken out of my hand.

" Now, Theo, how about those dances you promised me ? I'm just going to put my name down for them "—scribbling away on my card as he spoke.

" Nonsense, Willy ; give me back my card at once."

" No fear ; not till I've done with it. Well, this will do for a start," he said, at length returning me my card, black with his initials, and departing without giving me time to remonstrate. As he went away, Nugent came up.

" Can you give me a dance ? " he asked. " I am afraid it is not very likely, after the amount of time Willy has spent over your card. I never saw him write so much before in his life ; he looked as if he were writing a book."

" Oh, I think I have some left," I said, resolving to do as I thought fit about Willy's dances.

" Then, may I have 6, 11, 13, and 18, if you are here ; and supper ? "

" I am afraid I can't give you supper," I said,

glancing at the large " W " scrawled through the four supper extras on my card ; " but you can have the others, I think."

" Thanks ; that is very good of you. I think the next thing to be done is to ask Mrs. Croly for a waltz "—making a survey of the room as he spoke. " I always do, and she always pretends to strike me with her fan, and says, ' I suppose you're mistaking me for Sissie,' and is arch. I should watch if I were you ; I am sure you would like to see her looking arch."

I was, unfortunately, not privileged to see this phase of my hostess, as The O'Neill had already stationed himself beside me, so as not to lose a bar of his polka.

He danced with the determination peculiar to small fat men, and we stamped and curvetted round the room in circles so small that I found it difficult to keep on my feet.

" That wasn't bad," he gasped complacently, as we staggered to a corner and rested there, while he mopped his purple forehead. " You dance like a fairy, Miss Sarsfield. But, upon my soul, I think they get more pace on every year. That woman at the piano—Mrs. What's-her-name ? Whelply, isn't it ?—why, she's rattling away as if the devil was after her."

Looking about me, I saw with deep amusement that Willy had selected Miss Mimi Burke as his partner, and was charging with her through the throng at reckless speed. Her face, blazing with heat and excitement, showed no unworthy fears for her own safety ; and as, with her chin embedded in Willy's shoulder, they sped past, she cast an eye of exhilarated recognition at me.

" By Jove ! " wheezed O'Neill, still breathless from his exertions ; " old Mimi's got a wonderful kick in her gallop still ! She's getting over the ground like a three-year-old ! "

To me the appearance of my cousin and his partner was more suggestive of a large steamer going full speed through smaller craft, Miss Mimi's rubicund face representing the port light ; but I kept this brilliant idea to myself.

" I hope Willy knows how to steer," I said. " He does not take things so easily as your son appears to do."

Nugent was performing what was only too evidently a duty dance with one of the Misses Jackson-Croly—a very young lady, with fuzzy hair and a pink frock. They wound sadly along, as much as possible on the outskirts of the darting crowd, Nugent's expression of melancholy provoking his more agile parent to a laugh of mingled contempt and self-complacency.

" Take things easily ! " he repeated ; " why he's a regular muff. Who'd ever think he was a son of mine ? If *I* were dancing with a spicy little girl like that, I wouldn't look as if I were at my own funeral. Shall we have another turn ? " and before I had time for a counter suggestion we were again hopping and spinning round the room.

I had no reason to complain of lack of attention

on the part of my hostess, and I and my card were soon in a state of equal confusion. The generic name of Mrs. Jackson-Croly's " dancing gentlemen " appeared to be either Beamish or Barrett, and had it not been for Willy's elucidation of its mysteries, I should have thrown my card away in despair.

" No, not *him*. That's *Long* Tom Barrett ! It's *English* Tommy you're to dance with next. They call him English Tommy because, when his militia regiment was ordered to Aldershot, he said he was ' the first of his ancestors that was ever sent on foreign service.' "

Willy's dances with me were, during this earlier part of the evening, sandwiched with great regularity between those of the clans Beamish and Barrett, and I found him to be in every way a most satisfactory partner. He was in a state of radiant amiability, and proved himself of inestimable value as a chronicler of interesting facts about the company in general. He was, besides, strong and sure-footed—qualities, as I had reason to know, not to be despised in an assemblage such as this. I carried for several days the bruises which I received during my waltz with English Tommy. It consisted chiefly of a series of short rushes, of so shattering a nature that I at last ventured to suggest a less aggressive mode of progression.

" Well," said English Tommy, confidentially, " ye see, I'm trying to bump Katie ! That's Katie "— pointing to a fat girl in blue. " She's my cousin, and we're for ever fighting."

There seemed at the time nothing very incongruous about this explanation. There was a hilarious informality about the whole entertainment that made it unlike any I had ever been at before. Every one talked and laughed at the full pitch of their lungs. An atmosphere of utmost intimacy pervaded the assemblage, and Christian names and strange nicknames were bandied freely about among the groups in the corners. The music was supplied by volunteers from the ranks of the chaperons, at the end of each dance the musicians receiving a round of applause, varying in volume according to the energy and power of endurance displayed. The varieties of style and time thus attained were almost unimaginable, and were only equalled by the corresponding vagaries of the dancers, whose trampings and shufflings and runnings were as amazing as they were unexpected.

I could see Madam O'Neill sitting in state at the end of the room, surrounded by lesser matrons, her boredom only alleviated by the acute disfavour with which she viewed the revels.

" Do you know where Connie is, my dear ? " she said with pale asperity, as I came up to her after a dance. " I have not seen her for the last four dances."

I was well aware that Connie and Captain Forster had long since established themselves in the conservatory, but Madam O'Neill was too full of her grievance to give me time to reply.

" I am perfectly horrified at what you must think

of all this," she went on. "Even here I never saw such a noisy, romping set. You know, we are quite in the backwoods here—all the *nice* people live at the other end of the county—and you mustn't take these as specimens of Irish society."

I was spared the necessity of replying by the appearance of Nugent.

"Nugent, *where* is Connie?" demanded the Madam again. "It is too bad of her to make herself so remarkable in a place like this."

"Oh, she's all right; she's with Forster somewhere," he answered, with the incaution of total indifference. "Here's your host coming to take you in to supper, and I advise you to avoid the sherry. This is our dance, No. 11," he said to me. "We had better not lose any more of it."

CHAPTER XIX.

WE were at supper. The chaperons had at length completed their well-earned repast, and had returned, flushed and loquacious, to the dancing-room, yielding their places to the hungry throng who had been waiting outside the door.

The last waltz had been played by Miss Sissie Croly, in good time and with considerable spirit, an act of coquettish self-abnegation which elicited many tender reproaches from her forsaken partner. Making the most of the temporary improvement in the music, Nugent and I had danced without stopping, until a series of sensational flourishes announced that the end of the waltz was at hand. After it was over, he had suggested supper, and we had secured a small table at the end of the supper-room, from which, in comparative quiet, we could view the doings of the rest of the company. I was guiltily conscious of the large " W " scrawled across the supper extras on my card ; but a latent rebellion against my cousin's appropriation conspired with a distinct desire for food to harden my heart. I made up my mind to do what seemed good to me about one at least of the extras, and dismissed for the present all further thought of Willy and his possible grievances.

Meanwhile, the centre table was surrounded by what looked like a convivial party of lunatics. Miss Burke and Doctor Kelly had set the example of decorating themselves with the coloured paper caps contained in the crackers, and the other guests had instantly adopted the idea. Mob-caps, night-caps, fools'-caps and sun-bonnets nodded in nightmare array round the table, Miss Burke's long red face showing to great advantage beneath a pale-blue, tissue-paper tall hat.

" I feel I have been very remiss in not offering to pull a cracker with you," said Nugent, " but I am afraid they have all been used up by this time ! "

" Why did I not go in to supper with Doctor Kelly ? " I said regretfully. " If the worst came to the worst, I am sure he would have taken off his own sun-bonnet and put it on my head ! "

" Go in with him next time," suggested Nugent. " He always goes into supper two or three times, and works his way each time down the table like a mowing-machine, leaving nothing behind him. At the masonic ball in Cork he was heard saying to his sisters, as they were going in to supper, ' Stuff, ye divils ! there's ice ! ' "

" Quite right, too," I said, beginning upon the tipsy-cake which Nugent had looted for our private consumption. " I always make a point of stuffing when there is ice. However, I think on the whole I have had enough of Doctor Kelly for one evening.

I have danced once with him, and I suppose it is because he is at least a foot shorter than I am that he makes himself about half his height when he is dancing with me. But I think all small men do that ; the taller their partner, the more they bend their knees."

Nugent laughed. " I have been watching you dancing with all sorts and conditions of men, and wondering what you thought of them. I also wondered if you would find them sufficiently amusing to induce you to stay on till No. 18 ? " he said, putting his elbows on the table and looking questionably at me.

" Oh, I hope so—at least—of course, that depends on your mother," I answered.

" Should you care to stay ? "

" It would be better not to bother your mother about it, perhaps—of course, it might be very pleasant to stay," I answered confusedly.

The way in which he had asked the question had given me a strange sensation for a moment. " For one reason, I should like you to see what it gets like towards the end——"

I went on with the buttoning of my gloves without answering.

" And for another—I daresay it's not any argument —I shall be very sorry if you go."

His eyes were fixed on mine across the intervening woodcock and tipsy-cake with more inquiry than seemed necessary, but as he finished speaking a little troop of men came in together for a supplementary supper, and I forgot everything but my own guilt, as among them I saw Willy. It was evident that he had not come with any gluttonous intent, and, after a cursory look round the room over people's heads, he walked out.

"Did you see Willy?" I said, in a scared whisper.

"Yes, perfectly. He was probably looking for you."

"Oh, I know he was!" I said, beginning to gather up my fan and other belongings. "I ought to go at once. I am engaged to him for the extras."

"Are you afraid of Willy?" returned Nugent, without taking his elbows off the table, or making any move.

"No, of course I'm not. But I don't like to throw him over."

"Oh, I see!" he said, still without moving, and regarding me with an aggravating amusement.

"Well, *I* am going——" I began, when a hand was laid on my arm.

"I am delighted to hear it," said Connie's voice, "as we want this table. Get up, Nugent, and give me your chair. Nothing would induce me to sit at that bear-garden"—indicating the larger table. "What do you think I heard Miss Donovan say to that little Barrett man—English Tommy—as I was making my way up here? 'Now, captain, if you say that again, I'll pelt me patty at you!' And I haven't the least doubt that at this moment his shirt-front is covered with it."

"Oh, all right," said Nugent, slowly getting up, "you can have this table : we were just going. Miss Sarsfield is very anxious to find Willy. She says she is going to dance all the extras with him."

"Then she is rather late," replied Connie, unconcernedly. "Captain Forster, go *at once* and get me some game-pie. Don't tell me there's none ; I couldn't bear it. Well, my dear," she continued, "perhaps you are not aware that the extras are all over, and No. 12 is going on now ? "

"Have you seen Willy anywhere ? " I asked, feeling rather than seeing the sisterly eye of facetious insinuation that Connie directed at her brother. "I am engaged to him for No. 12."

"At this moment he is dancing with Miss Dennehy," answered Connie, "but I know he has been looking for you. He has prowled in and out of the conservatory twenty times."

"He was in here too," said Nugent ; "and I think he saw you," he added, as we walked into the hall. "What would you like to do now ? Willy has evidently thrown you over, and I expect my partner has consoled herself. I think the safest plan is to hide somewhere till this is over, and, as 13 is ours, we can then emerge, and dance it with blameless composure."

The doors of the conservatory at the end of the hall stood invitingly open, and a cool, fragrant waft of perfume came through them. Without further deliberation, we mutely accepted their invitation, and finding, by the dim, parti-coloured light of Chinese lanterns, that two arm-chairs had been placed at the further end, we immediately took possession of them.

"Occasionally rest is vouchsafed even to the wicked," said Nugent, leaning back, and picking up my fan, which I had laid on the floor, and beginning lazily to examine it. "Looking at a ball in the abstract, I think it involves great weariness and vexation of spirit. Out of twenty-four dances, there are at most four or five that one really looks forward to. You *are* going to stay for No. 18, you know," he added quietly. "I shall settle that with the Madam."

"Give me my fan, please," I said, taking no notice of this assertion. "I can see you know just the right way to break it."

He sat up, and, instead of returning it, began slowly to fan me. There was a brief silence. The rain pattered down on the glass overhead. We could just hear the music, and the measured stamping of the dancers' feet.

"Do you know," he said suddenly, "you are curiously different from what I expected you to be."

"Why? Had you formed any definite idea about me?"

"Not in the least. That was what threw me so out of my reckoning. I thought I knew pretty well, in a general way, what you were going to be like; but somehow you have made me reconstruct all my notions."

"If you had only told me in time, I should have tried to be less inconsiderate. It is so painful to have to give up one's ideas."

"I did not find it so," he said seriously; "on the contrary. I wonder"—continuing to flap my fan to and fro—"if you ever had a kind of latent ideal—a sort of thing which seems so impossible that you never try to form any very concrete theory about it? I suppose it very seldom happens to a man to find that an idea he has only dreamt about is a real thing after all. Can you imagine what an effect it would have upon him when he found that he had unexpectedly met his—well, his ideal?"

He folded up the fan, and looked down at me, waiting for an answer.

"I should imagine he would think himself very clever," I said, feeling rather nervous.

"No, not clever, I don't think, so much as fortunate; that is to say"—he drew a short breath—"of course the ideal may have ideas of her—of its own that the man can't live up to—independent schemes, in fact; and then—why, then that man gets left, you know," he ended, with a change of tone.

As he finished speaking, the far-off banging of the piano ceased. I did not know how to reply to what he had said; I was not even sure of what he had meant, and while I sat awkwardly silent, the dancers came crowding into the conservatory, all in turn exhibiting the same resentful surprise, as they found the only chairs occupied. Willy was not among them, nor did I see him during the ensuing dance, and, as his late partner was in the room, I could only conclude that he was sitting out by himself. I began to feel unhappy about him, and half dreaded meeting him again. The dance seemed interminably long. I kept my eyes fixed on the door to see if he were among the string of black and red-coated men who wandered partnerless in and out, but could see no sign of him. Nugent was silent and preoccupied, and it was almost a relief to me when at length the music ceased.

"It is very strange that I do not see Willy anywhere," I said, as we came out into the hall again.

"Who? Oh! Willy," he said. "Are you still looking for him? Is not that he coming out of the supper-room?"

It *was* Willy. I dropped Nugent's arm. "I must speak to him for a minute," I said hurriedly. "I want to explain to him——"

By this time Willy had met us, and looked as if he were going to pass me by.

"Do you know that this is our dance?" I said, stopping him. "You are not going to throw me over again, are you?" My heart beat rather fast as I made this feeble endeavour to carry the war into the enemy's country. He was looking grey and ill, and I did not think that his pleasant face could have taken on such an expression of gloomy coldness.

"Really? Is it? I did not know that I was to

have the honour of dancing with you again," he responded, with a boyish attempt at frigid dignity.

"Of course it is," I said cheerily, though I felt rather alarmed. "Look at it in black and white."

Willy did not look at the card which I held towards him.

"It doesn't appear that my name being written there makes much difference," he answered, making a movement as if to pass on.

"Oh, Willy, that isn't fair! You know I danced ever so often with you before supper, and afterwards I was looking for you everywhere; was I not, Mr. O'Neill?"—turning for corroboration to Nugent. He, however, had left me to fight my own battles, and was at a little distance, deep in conversation with Mr. Dennehy. I saw that, whether verified or not, my explanation had but little effect upon Willy, and I boldly assumed the offensive. "You know, I never said that I was going to give you all those dances that you took."

"Of course you were at perfect liberty to do what you liked about them," returned Willy, without looking at me.

"Don't be absurd! You know quite well what I mean, and if you had wanted to dance with me you might very easily have found me. I was only in the supper-room."

He said nothing, and just then we heard the first few notes of the next waltz.

"You *will* dance this with me, won't you?" I said, thoroughly unhappy at the turn things were taking.

" I am very sorry. I didn't think you would mind. Don't be angry with me, Willy," I ended impulsively, putting my hand into his arm.

He looked at me almost wildly for a moment ; and then, without a word, we joined the stream of dancers who were returning to the ball-room.

CHAPTER XX.

MRS. JACKSON-CROLY'S party had reached its climax of success.

"The supper's put great heart into them," little Doctor Kelly remarked confidentially to Willy, as he passed us, leading a stout elderly matron forth to dance. The chaperons, with but few exceptions, had abandoned the hard chairs and narrow sofas on which they had hitherto huddled in chilly discomfort, and were, again to quote Dr. Kelly, "footing it with the best of them."

Mrs. Croly herself was playing "Sweethearts," and by way, as I suppose, of receiving this favour with proper enthusiasm, the guests, as they danced, sang the words of the refrain—

> Oh, lo—*ove* for a year,
> A we—*eek*, a day,

as often as it recurred, Mrs. Croly from the piano lending her powerful aid to swell the chorus. Madam O'Neill was sitting alone upon her sofa, and had closed her eyes during this later development of the entertainment, whether in real or simulated slumber I did not know; but an expressive glance from

Connie, whom, to my surprise, I saw circling in the arms of our host, told me that the latter was more probably the case. The O'Neill I had lately espied sitting in an arm-chair on the landing of the stairs with a very pretty young lady, the instructress of the younger Misses Jackson-Croly. He, at all events, was enjoying himself, and as far as he was concerned I felt none of the qualms of conscience at the lateness of the hour which assailed me at sight of my chaperon's tired face.

Willy had not spoken since we had begun to dance, but I thought it best to behave as if nothing were the matter.

" This is the most amusing dance I ever was at in my life," I said, in the first pause that we made.

" I don't see much difference between it and any other."

" I don't mean to say that I have not enjoyed myself," I said, anxious to avoid any semblance of superiority, " but you must admit that one does not usually meet people who are able to sing and dance a waltz at the same time."

At this point there came a sudden thud on the floor, followed by a slight commotion.

" Hullo ! Croly's let Connie down ! " exclaimed Willy, forgetting for an instant his offended dignity.

I was just in time to catch between the dancers a glimpse of Connie struggling, hot and angry, to her feet, while her partner lay prone on his back on the floor. The catastrophe had taken place just in front of Madam O'Neill, whose eyes, now wide open, were bent in a gaze of petrified indignation on Mr. Jackson-Croly. Nugent had not been dancing, and, on seeing Connie fall, had gone round to pick her up, and now made his way towards me.

" Did you see them come down ? " he said. " Croly hung on to Connie like a drowning man to a straw, and Connie, not being exactly a straw, nearly drove his head into the floor. She won't speak to him now, which is rather hard luck, considering she all but killed him ! Wasn't I right in advising you to stay on till the end ? "

Exceeding laughter had deprived me of all power of speech, but, in any case, Willy did not give me time to reply.

" Come out of this," he said roughly ; " I'm sick of it." He gave me his arm as he spoke, and elbowed his way past Nugent out of the room. He walked without speaking through the hall towards the conservatory, but stopped short at the door. " It's full of people in there. Croly's study's the only place where you've a chance of being let alone," he said, turning down a passage, and leading the way into a dreary little room, lighted by a smoky paraffin lamp and pervaded by the odour of tobacco and whisky. On the inky table, two or three tumblers with spoons in them, and a bottle and decanter, were standing in shining patches of spilt whisky and water. A few office chairs were drawn up in front of the remains of a smouldering turf fire. Long files of bills hung beside an old coat on some pegs, and Mr. Croly's cloth slippers showed modestly from under a small horsehair sofa. A more untempting place to sit in could not well be imagined ; but Willy did not seem to notice its discomforts. He sat down on one of the chairs, and began aimlessly to poke the fire ; while I, gingerly drawing my skirts together, established myself on the sofa.

" I can't say I think this an improvement on the conservatory," I said at length, seeing that Willy did not seem inclined to talk. " When did you discover it ? "

He threw down the poker, and, standing up, began to examine a specimen of ore that lay on the chimney-piece.

" If you want to know particularly," he said, in a hard and would-be indifferent voice, " I came and sat in here by myself while those extras were going on."

" That wasn't a very cheerful thing to do."

" Well, I didn't feel very cheerful," he answered, still with his back to me, and beginning to scrape the marble mantelshelf with the piece of ore which he held in his hand.

" Some one appears to have found a certain solace here," I said, looking at the whisky and water. " I am sure poor Mr. Croly has crept in from time to time, and put on his old coat and slippers, and tried to forget that there was a dance going on in his house."

No answer from Willy.

" Then perhaps it was *you*," I continued, with ill-assumed levity. " I am sorry to think that you have taken to such evil courses."

He went on hammering at the chimney-piece without replying.

"It's very rude of you not to answer; and you are ruining Mr. Croly's mantel-piece."

He put down the piece of ore suddenly, and, leaving the fireplace, came and stood over me.

"Theo!" he said, in a breathless sort of way, and stopped. I looked up at him with quick alarm, and saw that he was trying to get mastery enough over himself to speak. "Don't look at me like that," he said, almost in a whisper. "I'm nearly mad as it is. I can't bear it any longer; I must say it."

"Don't, Willy," I said; "please don't. It would be better for us both if you didn't."

"I don't care," he said, kneeling down beside me, and taking hold of both my hands. "You've got to listen to me now. You needn't think that I don't know I haven't a chance. I've seen that plain enough to-night, if I didn't know it before. Oh, I know, Theo; I know very well," he ended brokenly.

I could find nothing to say. I liked him so much that I could not bring myself to frame the truth which he would have to hear. I suppose my silence encouraged him, for in the same breathless abrupt way he went on.

"I know I'm an ignorant brute; but if you would only just try me. Oh, Theo, if you could only know! I'm such a fool I can't get hold of the right words to tell you, but you might believe me all the same. Indeed I do love you—I love you," he repeated, with a sort of sob, gathering both my hands into one of his and kissing them passionately.

"Willy," I said despairingly, trying to free my hands from his grasp, "you must stop ; you make me miserable. I can't bear to hear you talk like that. You know how much I like you and respect you, and everything. I am fonder of you than any one I know almost, but not in that way."

"But if you were fond of me at all, I wouldn't mind how little you liked me at first, if you'd let me care for you. May-be it would come to you afterwards ; and you know the governor would like it awfully," said the poor boy, lifting his white face, and gazing at me with desperate eyes.

"It's no use, Willy ; I can't let you say any more about it. I'm not worth your caring for me like that," I said unsteadily.

His hands relaxed their grasp, and, drawing mine away, I stood up. He got up also, and stood facing me in the smoky light of the lamp. He leaned his hand on the table beside him, and the ringing of the spoons and glasses told me how it trembled. When he next spoke, however, his voice was firmer.

"That's no answer. You're worth more to me than everything in the world. If it was only *that* "— with a shaky laugh—" but I know that's not your reason. Look here—will you tell me one thing ? "— coming closer, and staring hard at me. "Is it another fellow ? Is it—is it Nugent ? "

"It is nothing of the kind," I said angrily, but at the same time flushing hotly under his scrutiny.

" You have no right to say such things. If I had never seen him, I should feel just the same towards you."

I turned to take my bouquet from the sofa with the intention of leaving the room, but before I could do so, Willy snatched it up, and, taking a stride forward, he flung the flowers into the fire, and crushed them with his foot into the burning embers.

" How dare you, Willy ! " I said, thoroughly roused. " What right had you to do that ? "

" And what right have *you* to say you don't care for him, when you carry his cursed flowers in your hand ? I see how the land lies well enough. I've been made a fool of all through ! "

" You have not been made a fool of," I said, with equal energy. " It is cruel of you to say that."

" Cruel ? It comes well from you to say that ! I dare say you think it doesn't matter much ; but maybe some day, when I've gone to the devil, you'll be sorry."

He walked to the door, as if to go.

" I *am* sorry, Willy," I said, the tears rushing to my eyes. " Don't go away like that. Oh, why did I ever come to Durrus ? "

He stood irresolute for a moment, with the handle of the door in his hand, looking at me as if in a daze. Then, with an inarticulate exclamation, he came back to where I was standing, and, before I had time to stop him, took me in his arms. I was too much unstrung and exhausted by what had gone before to resist, and I stood in a kind of horror of passive endurance while he kissed me over and over again. He let me go at last.

" It's no use," he said, in a choked voice, which sounded almost like a groan ; " it's no use." His eye fell on the bunch of violets in my dress. " Give them to me," he whispered.

I silently took out of my dress the bunch he had given me, and handed them, all limp and faded, to him. He took them without looking at me, and, turning his back to me, walked to the chimney-piece. He leaned both his arms upon the narrow shelf, and laid his head upon them.

When I left the room, he was still standing motionless in the same position.

CHAPTER XXI.

THE old graveyard on the promontory was at most times the forlornest and least frequented spot about Durrus. The dead people who lay in crowded slumber within the grey, briar-covered walls seldom heard any disturbing human voice to remind them of the life they had left. Their solitude was ensured to them by the greater solitude of the sea, which on three sides surrounded them, and by the dreary strip of worn-out turf bog which formed their only link with the rest of the world. There was nothing to mark for them the passing of time except the creeping of the shadow thrown dial-wise by the gable of the broken-down chapel, or the ever-increasing moaning in the caves beneath, which told of the yearly encroachments of the sea.

Between the verge of the cliff and the wall of the graveyard was only a narrow space, along which the sheep had worn themselves a track among the thickly lying shells and *débris*, flung up by the waves during autumn storms. I had wandered round this narrow path, holding with a careful hand to the wall as I went ; and now had clambered on to it, and, with Pat seated in my lap and Jinny on the tail of my gown, I was watching the quick dives and casual reappearances of the slim black cormorants in the sunlit water beneath me. The murmur of the sea, lightly lipping the rocks, and an occasional bleat from the sheep in the graveyard behind me, were the only definite sounds I heard, and the soft wind that rustled in my ears in little gusts seemed the expression of the pervading stillness.

This delicate breezy morning was the first of the new year. Yesterday's sunset had been a wild one ; it had gleamed angrily and fitfully before me through packs of jagged cloud while I drove home from Clashmore, and my heart had sunk low as I watched the outlines of Durrus growing darker against it. But that was already a thing of last year. The long uneventful darkness had made everything new, and on this first of January the sunshine was lying purely and dreamily on sea and bog, and was even giving something like warmth to the head-stones, whose worn " Anno Dominis " were since yesterday more remote by a year.

It was a desire for this freedom and freshness which had driven me out of the house on this, the second morning after the dance at Mount Prospect. When I came back to Durrus the evening before, I had found the house empty and desolate. Willy was not there ; he had gone to Cork, Uncle Dominick had told me, looking at me, as he spoke, with a questioning glance that showed me his anxiety to know if I could account for this unexpected move.

All the morning at Clashmore the thought of the

inevitable meeting with Willy had hung over me. It had made me absent during a lesson at billiards, and stupid in a violin accompaniment ; and, combining with the guilt which I felt at enjoying myself, as, in spite of what had happened, I could not help doing, it had made me unnecessarily and awkwardly determined in refusing several invitations to stay on. As I sat beside Nugent in the dog-cart on the way home, and felt that every step of the horse was bringing me nearer to Willy, I had become silent in the attempt to nerve myself for the dreaded first few minutes. If I could struggle through them creditably, things might not afterwards be so bad. I think Nugent must have seen that something was troubling me. Having told me that he was afraid I was very much done up by the dance, he had considerately left me to myself, and scarcely spoke until we were at the Durrus hall door—an act of thoughtfulness for which I could almost have thanked him. He refused my invitation to come in to tea—an invitation so faintly given that he could hardly have accepted it—but asked if he might come over some other afternoon, perhaps the day after to-morrow, and with an excuse for not coming in, which he had obviously fabricated to help me out of the difficulty, he had driven away.

My first question to Roche as the hall door closed behind me, was to know where Willy was. He was away ; he had gone to Cork that morning, and it was uncertain when he would be at home. Then I might have stayed at Clashmore after all— that, I am afraid, was my first thought ; and then came the feeling of blank collapse, the blending of relief and disappointment, which is the usual result of needless mental strain. I had for an instant an insane desire to run down the avenue after the dog-cart, and say that I would go back to Clashmore ; that there was no reason now——I laughed drearily to myself as I took off my wraps. What would Nugent have said when I had overtaken him with such an excuse ? It amused me to think of it ; but yet, I thought, I should have liked to have known.

The restlessness of over-fatigue and excitement was upon me. I did not know how to endure the long dull dinner, and the solitary evening which followed it. I tried to play the piano, but the tunes of the waltzes of the night before still rang in my ears, and the unresponsive silence of the room as I ceased was too daunting to be faced a second time. Between my eyes and the columns of the newspaper came a vision of Mr. Croly's dark little room, and my tired brain kept continually framing sentences which might have averted all that had taken place there. I could not even think connectedly, and finally went to bed, as lonely and miserable as I have ever felt in my life.

In the morning my thoughts had confusedly shaped themselves into one problem. Would it be possible to go on staying at Durrus ? Half the morning had slipped away, and I had still found no answer to the question. My head ached, and I felt I could come to no decision until I was, for the present at least, out of the depressing atmosphere of the house.

I put the perplexing subject away from me in my

half-hour's walk across the bog, and thought of the
dogs, the sea-gulls, the patches of white cloud and
blue sky that seemed so out of place reflected in
the black pools by the side of the road—of anything,
in fact, rather than the difficulty which was troubling
me. I thought that when I got to the edge of the
cliffs, with nothing but the open sea before me, I
should be able to take a steadier view of the whole
position.

But I had been sitting in perfect tranquillity for
half an hour, and yet no inspiration had been brought
to me on the breath of the west wind that was coming
softly over the sea from America. " I suppose I
ought to go back to Aunt Margaret," was my last,
as it had been my first, thought ; " but it will be
very hard to have to leave Ireland. Besides, if I
go away now, Willy will think that I am going out
of kindness to him, and I could not bear that."

Here Pat, who had found the distant observation
of the cormorants a very tantalising amusement,
looked up in my face with a whimpering sigh, and
curled himself up with his head on my arm and his
back to the sea. As I stooped over and kissed his
little white and tan head, a crowd of insistent mem-
ories rushed into my mind. In every one Willy's
was the leading figure ; his look, his laugh, his voice
pervaded them all, but with a new meaning that made
pathos of the pleasantest of them. I wondered, with
perhaps some insincerity, why I had not liked him as
well as he liked me. He had said that, if I were to
try, I might some day ; but though I should have

been glad for his sake to believe it, every feeling in me rose in sudden revolt at the idea with a violence that astonished myself. "We shall never have any good times again," I thought. "I suppose he is miserable now, and it is all my fault. Oh, Willy! I never meant to be unkind to you," I ended, almost aloud, and the bright reaches of sea quivered and dazzled in my eyes as the painful tears gathered and fell.

I have always found that tears rather intensify a trouble than lessen it, and they now gave such keen reality to what I was feeling that I could bear the pressure of my thoughts no longer. I got up quickly to go home, and as I turned I saw a string of three or four boats heading for the little strand at the foot of the cliff, just below where I was standing. They were the cumbrous rowing-boats generally used for carrying turf, and came heavily on through the bright restless water, loaded, as well as I could see, with men and women.

The pounding and creaking of the clumsy oars in the rowlocks grew louder; I was soon able to make out that the long dark object, round which several figures were clustered in the leading boat, was a coffin, and I now remembered that Willy had told me that this little cove was called "Tra-na-morruf," the Strand of the Dead, from the fact that it was the landing-place for such funerals as came by boat to the old burying-place. The people were quite silent as the boats slowly advanced to the shore; but directly the keel of the first touched the shingle, the women in the others raised a sustained, penetrating wail, which rose and fell in the sunny air, and made me shiver in involuntary sympathy.

I thought I had never heard so terrible a cry. I had often been told of the Irish custom of " keening " at funerals, but I was not prepared for anything so barbaric and so despairing. It broke out with increasing volume and intensity while the coffin was being lifted from the boat and was toilfully carried up the steep path in the cliff, the women clapping their hands and beating their breasts, their chant rising and swelling like the howl of the wind on a wild night. The small procession halted at the top of the cliff, and another set of bearers took the coffin, and carried it with staggering steps across the irregular mounds of the graveyard, to where, behind the ruined chapel, I now noticed, for the first time, an open grave. The dark crowd closed in round it, and, after a few stifled sobs and exclamations, I heard nothing but the shovelling of the earth upon the coffin.

It was soon over. The throng of heavily cloaked women and frieze-coated men opened out, and I saw the long mound of brown earth, with a couple of women and a man kneeling beside it. The rest, for the most part, made their way down the cliff to the strand, from which a clatter of conversation soon ascended. About half a dozen of the women, however, remained behind ; each sought out some special grave, and, kneeling there, began to tell her beads and pray with seemingly deep devotion.

I moved away from where I had been standing,

with the intention of going home, but stopped at the gateway to look again at the effect of the black figures dotted about among the grey stones, with their background of pale blue sky. Near the gate was the ugly squat mausoleum in which lay many generations of Sarsfields, and as I passed through the gate I saw, kneeling at the farther side of it, a mourner dressed like the others in a hooded blue cloak. She was clapping her hands and beating her breast as if keening, but she made no sound. A country woman at this moment passed me, curtsying as she did so, and, feeling a natural curiosity to know who had taken upon herself the office of bewailing my ancestors, I said—

" Can you tell me who that woman at the Sarsfield tomb is ? "

" Faith, then, I can, your honour, miss ! But sure yourself should know her as well as me. 'Tis Moll Hourihane, that lives below at the lodge of the big house."

" Oh yes, of course, so it is," I said, recognising her as I spoke ; " but what has she come here for ? "

" Throth, I dunno, miss. But there's never a buryin' here that she's not at it, and that's the spot where she'll always post herself. Sure she's idioty-like ; she thinks she's keening there, and the divil a screech out of her, good or bad, all the time."

My informant gave a short laugh. She was a tall, handsome woman, with a strong Spanish type of face and daring black eyes, and she had a grimly humorous manner.

" Why does she pick out the Durrus tomb ? " I asked, as much to continue the conversation as for any other reason.

" Glory be to God, miss ! how would I know ? "— darting at me, however, a look of extreme intelligence, combined with speculation as to the extent of my ignorance. " 'Twas she laid out the owld masther afther he dying, whatever—yis, an' young Mrs. Dominick too. Though, fegs ! the sayin' is, she cried more for her whin she was alive than whin she was dead."

We were walking slowly along the uneven bog road towards Durrus, my companion trudging sociably beside me, with her hood thrown back from her coarse black hair.

" What do you mean ? " I said, hoping to hear at last something of the origin of Moll's madness.

" There's many a wan would cry if they got the turn out," she responded oracularly.

" Why, what was she turned out of ? " I asked.

" Out of the big house, sure ! 'Twas there she was till the young misthriss came."

" I suppose she was a servant there ? "

She gave a loud laugh. " Och ! 'twasn't thrusting to being a servant at all she was ! She was in it ever and always till Misther Dominick got marri'd, and then, faith, she had to quit."

I was rather puzzled.

" I suppose Mrs. Sarsfield liked to choose her servants for herself."

The woman gave a derisive snort. " It 'ud be a

quare thing if she'd choose *her* whatever!" she said. "Annyway, she never came next or nigh the house till after Mrs. Dominick dyin', and thin she was took back to mind the owld masther and Masther Willy."

"But I thought she was weak in her head?"

"Och! the divil a fear! She was as 'cute as a pet fox till the winther the owld masther died; but whatever came agin her thin I don't rightly know. 'Twas about the time she marri'd Michael Brian it began with her. She looked smart enough; but the spaych mostly went from her, and she was a year that way." Here she looked behind her, and crossed herself with a start. "The saints be about us!" she exclaimed, in a whisper; "look at herself follying us!"

I also turned, and saw Moll Hourihane close behind. She was walking on the strip of grass by the side of the road, and, without looking at us, she passed by, moving with a sliding shuffle. She hurried along in front of us until she came near the gate in the Durrus avenue, when she left the road and turned aside into the bog. She made her way across it until her farther progress was stopped by the turf-boat dyke. Turning, like a dog on a trail, she followed its course till stopped again by the dyke that met it at right angles. There, opposite the old turf-quay, she knelt, and folding her hands on her breast, as she had done on the first night I had seen her, she remained there without moving.

"Look at her now," said my companion, superstitiously, " saying her prayers there down by the wather, as if 'twas before the althar she was. Faith, whin she had her sinses she wasn't so great at her prayers ! "

" I suppose that place is deep enough to drown her ? " I said, regarding it and her with exceeding disfavour.

" Is it Poul-na-coppal ? Sure it's the deepest hole in the country ! Wasn't it there a fine young horse backed down in it one time, and a car o' turf on him, and they never seen the sight of him again, nor the car o' turf nayther ! There's no bottom in it, only mud. Throth ! if she got in there she'd stay in it ; and it'd be a good job if she did too—God forgive me for sayin' such a thing ! "

" Don't you think we ought to try and get her away from there ? " I said, still watching Moll with a kind of fascination, as she rocked herself to and fro close to the edge.

" Wisha, thin, I'd be in dhread to go near her at all. Faith ! there's times when she wouldn't be said nor led by her own daughther."

" It was after Anstey was born that she went completely out of her mind, wasn't it ? " I said, as we walked on.

" Well, 'twas thin the sinse left her entirely, miss ; but she wasn't all out right in her head, as I'm tellin' ye, for a year before that. There was a big snow came afther the little gerr'l was born, and they say, whin she seen that she let one bawl out of her, and never spoke a word afther, nor put a hand to the child, good nor bad. And indeed poor Anstey's a good little gerr'l. 'Tis the Brians—that's the father's family—she favours entirely, and the Brians was nice quiet people always."

We had by this time come to the little gate that led out of the bog.

" Good-evening to your honour, miss. May the Lord comfort your honour long, and that I may never die till I see you well married," with which comprehensive benediction and an impressive curtsy my companion tramped off down the avenue.

I felt lonelier for the cessation of her rough, vigorous voice ; and, turning, I leaned on the gate, and looked back over the sunshiny bleakness of the bog. It looked now very much as it had looked on the day when I had gone out to see Willy put Alaska through her paces, and as the fragrant wind brought the sea murmurs to me, I almost cheated myself into the belief that this was still that brilliant October afternoon, and that Willy was now riding down to meet me at the lodge.

My eyes fell on the solitary figure down by the dyke. It recalled in a moment the funeral, the graveyard, my futile tears, and all that had led to them. I turned towards home with the same feeling of uncertainty and dejection with which I had set out.

CHAPTER XXII.

" No news from Willy ? I thought *you* would have been sure to have heard from him."

" No, Uncle Dominick, he never even told me he was going," I replied, with a full consciousness of the emphasis laid on the " you."

" Really ! How very strange ! I thought Master Willy seldom did anything nowadays without consulting a certain young lady."

I went on with my lunch without speaking. These pleasantries on my uncle's part were not uncommon, and, as there was no mistaking whither they all tended, I hated and dreaded them more every day. In this particular instance, I believed I saw very plainly a real anxiety to find out the state of affairs between Willy and me, and I thought it best to hold my tongue. My silence did not discourage Uncle Dominick.

" I forgot to tell you last night that I met Miss Burke yesterday," he said. " She gave me a great deal of news about the ball, and told me that every one said that you and Willy were ' the handsomest couple in the room.' I told her that as far as one of you was concerned I could well believe it ; and, indeed, Willy is not such a bad-looking fellow, after all, eh ? "

" I think Miss Burke herself and Willy were a much more striking pair," I answered, evading the question, and anxious to show him that I disliked the way in which I was for ever bracketed with Willy. " Oh, by the way, Uncle Dominick," I went on, regardless of a conviction that I was saying the wrong thing, " I heard from Mr. O'Neill this morning. He says that he is coming over here this afternoon, to fetch some music which he left here the other day."

Uncle Dominick gave me a sharp look from under his bushy eyebrows. It was one of those unguarded glances which, for the moment, strip the face of all conventional disguises, and lay bare all that is hidden of suspicion and surmise. I noticed suddenly how bloodshot his eyes were, and how very pale he was looking. There was dead silence. By way of appearing unconscious and indifferent, I took out of my pocket Nugent's letter, and began to read it ; but I felt in every fibre that my uncle was watching me, and a maddening blush slowly mounted to my forehead, and spread itself even to the tips of my ears. Uncle Dominick cleared his throat with ominous severity, and pushed back his chair from the table.

" At what hour do you expect Mr. O'Neill ? "

If he had asked me at what time in the afternoon I contemplated committing a burglary, he could not have spoken with more concentrated disapproval.

" I have not the least idea," I said, getting up with as much dignity as I could muster. " I suppose about the time people usually come."

" H'm ! I suppose one cannot expect young ladies to be very lucid in their statements about such matters," he replied, with a singularly unpleasant smile.

" I suppose not," I retorted obstinately.

" Well, I suppose one must only expect him when he comes," said my uncle, with a return of suavity, as distasteful to me as his former manner. I called the dogs away from their assiduous polishing of the plates on which they had had their dinners, and left him to finish his wine alone.

" How detestable he can be when he likes ! " I thought, seating myself before the drawing-room fire. " I wonder why he dislikes Nugent so much ? I don't suppose it can be on account of Willy ; after all, there is really no reason for that." My cheeks were still hot, and I put my hands over them, looking through my fingers into the fire. " If Uncle Dominick is going to make himself unpleasant in this kind of way, I shall have to go back to Canada no matter what Willy thinks about it."

My ideas as to leaving Durrus were still as hazy as they had been yesterday morning at the old graveyard, and this was a fresh complication. I had, however, made up my mind on one point—until I saw Willy again, I would settle nothing. That was at least definite ; and so was the fact which at this moment occurred to me—that I should break down in one of the more difficult of the violin accompaniments if I did not practise it before Nugent came. I gave the fire an impatient poke, and, mentally throwing my reflections into it, went over to the piano.

I had said to my uncle that I supposed Nugent would come at the usual time, but I was forced to the conclusion that his views on the subject differed from those of most people. Tea-time came, and, after waiting till the tea was bitter, and the buttered toast half congealed, I partook of it in solitude. I began to wonder if it were possible that he could have made a mistake about the day, and again taking out his letter, I read it over. The strong handwriting was not that of a person who made mistakes, and it set forth plainly the fact that on this afternoon the writer intended to come and see me, and would come as early as he could. The sprawling minute-hand of the ormolu clock was now well on its way towards half-past five ; something must have happened to prevent him from coming, unless, indeed, he had forgotten all about it. I did not think it likely that he would forget, but the possibility was not a pleasant one. I sat in the cheery light of the fire until the minute-hand had passed the illegibly ornamental figure which marked the half-hour, and, feeling a good deal more disappointed than I cared to own to myself, I was going to ring for the lamp and settle down to a book, when I heard the sound of quick trotting, and the light run of a dog-cart's wheels on the avenue.

" I know I'm very late," said Nugent, as he shook hands with me, " and I meant to be very early, but it wasn't my fault. I am sure you are going to tell me that the tea is cold, but I don't care ; I prefer it with the chill just off."

" Then you will be gratified," I said, pouring it out. " I began to think you were not coming, and was repenting that I had wasted half an hour in practising that awful accompaniment of Brahms'."

" Did you really ? It was very good of you. I did my best to get away early, but I had to stay and see Captain Forster off. I can't say that he seemed to appreciate the attention, as he was out for a walk with Connie up to the last minute. I was very sorry afterwards that I had been such a fool as to lose the whole afternoon on his account."

" I think you might have left him in Connie's hands," I said, sociably beginning upon a second edition of tea.

" I want to know if you are all right again," said Nugent, looking at me scrutinisingly. " I thought you seemed awfully played out the day before yesterday."

" Did I ? " I said. " I wasn't in the least—I mean I was very tired, but that was all."

" You scarcely spoke to me all the way over here. I don't know if you generally treat people like that when you are very tired."

" No," I said ; " when I know people well enough, I am simply cross."

" That means that you don't know me very well."

" No, I don't think I do," I said, with unpremeditated truthfulness. " By the way, is it true that you are all going away from Clashmore soon ? You said something about it in your letter."

" Yes ; I believe they are all off next week," he replied ; " but I think I shall stay on here for a bit. I don't want to go away just now."

I was on the point of saying that I was very glad to hear he was going to stay, but stopped myself, and said instead that I should have thought he would find it rather dreary by himself.

" I don't expect I shall," he answered. " I shall ask you to let me come over here very often. You know we agreed at Clashmore that you were to take my music in hand, and teach me to count."

" If I try to do that, we shall certainly have plenty of occupation," I said, laughing at the prospect with a foolish enjoyment.

" All right, so much the better "—looking at me and laughing too. " By the way, Connie wants to know if you will ride over to Mount Prospect with her and me the day after to-morrow, to pay our respects after the dance."

" I shall be very glad, I have not had a ride for a long time. Should you mind ringing the bell ? We shall want the lamps for the piano."

" I should mind very much," he said, without moving from the substantial arm-chair in which he was sitting. " I think it would be a much better scheme to sit over the fire instead. You were in such an extraordinary hurry to get away from Clashmore

the day before yesterday, that you did not give
me time for more than half the clever things I had
prepared to say about the Jackson-Crolys' dance."

"Very well," I said, dragging out a little old-
fashioned, glass-beaded footstool, and settling myself
comfortably with my feet on it in front of the fire.
"You can begin now, and say them all one after the
other ; but you needn't try to be clever. Nothing
that any one could invent could be half as amusing
as the truth ! "

"You must not fancy that all our county Cork
entertainments are on the Mount Prospect pattern,"
he said, anxiously. "I dare say you think we are
all savages, but we don't often have a war-dance
like that."

"Well," I said, checking an inclination to sigh
as the thought crossed my mind, "I shall always
be glad that I saw at least one before I went back
to Canada."

He got up and put down his cup ; then, drawing his
unwieldy chair closer to me before sitting down, "But
you are not thinking of going back to Canada ?" he
said slowly.

"Oh ! well, of course I shall have to go back
sooner or later," I replied, as airily as I could. "I
don't mean to spend my whole life here."

"Don't you ?" he said, in a low voice, leaning forward and trying to intercept my eyes, as I looked
straight before me into the fire. "I wish you would
tell me if you really mean that."

"I certainly do mean it," I answered, with decision. "And, after all, I can't see that it much matters whether I do or not."

"Why do you say it doesn't matter?" he said slowly.

"Oh, I don't know," I answered idiotically.

"But I think you ought to know before you make assertions of that kind," he persisted. "I dare say there are several people who would think it mattered a good deal."

He spoke with an intention in his voice that I had never heard before.

My heart paused, as if a hand had clutched it. Did he mean Willy?

"Don't you remember my telling you the other night of one person who had changed his mind? Have you quite forgotten what I said to you then?"

He was very near to me, so near that he must almost have felt my breath as it quickly came and went. My heart was beating fast enough now— hurrying along at such speed that I could not be sure enough of my voice to speak.

"Can you not think of any one to whom it would make a good deal of difference if you went back to Canada? Couldn't you?" He hesitated. "Don't you know it would make all the difference in the world to—to me?"

His hand found mine, and, as it closed upon it, I felt in one magical moment that there was but one hand in the world whose touch could send that strange pang of delight through me. His eyes lifted mine to them in spite of me. I do not know what he read in them, but in his I thought I saw something quite new—something that made me giddy, and took away my power of speaking.

"Don't you know it?" he whispered. "Theo——"

He stopped at the sound of a footstep outside the door. I recognised it in an instant.

"Here is Willy!" I gasped. The door opened, letting in a blaze of light, and Willy, followed by Roche with a lamp, came into the room.

The necessity of the moment gave me a fictitious courage. Pushing back my chair, I jumped up to meet him with an ease and cordiality intended to cover his embarrassment and my own.

"So here you are back, Willy! We have been wondering what had become of you."

He did not look at me as we shook hands, but he answered, in a voice as successfully friendly as my own :—

"I was forced to go up to Cork on business. I thought I could get down last night, but I couldn't manage it. How are you, Nugent?" he went on stiffly. "You'll have a pretty wet drive home. It was pouring when I came in."

Nugent at once took the hint thus broadly given.

"Yes, I dare say I shall," he said coolly. "Would you order my trap, please?"—turning to Roche, who had not yet left the room. "Good-night, Miss Sarsfield. Does that ride hold good?"

"I beg your pardon, Sir," put in Roche, "the masther says he'd be glad to see you before you go."

" All right," said Nugent.

He took my hand in his, and held it with a strong pressure.

" Then you'll come ? "

Something weighed down my eyelids—I could not meet his eyes again, and I answered hurriedly :—

" Yes—oh yes, I hope so ! Good-night."

CHAPTER XXIII.

I THINK I must have been very deficient in the power of self-analysis. I had always taken my life as it came, without much introspective thought of its effect upon me, and on the one or two occasions when I had been confronted with the necessity for knowing my own mind, I had never found the need for searchings of heart to discover if the germs of any unsuspected feelings were hidden there. I had taken for granted that I must be a hard-headed, hard-hearted person ; I used to listen with an amused sympathy to the intricacies of sentimental detail with which many of my friends recounted their experiences, and I had often offered, not without a certain sense of superiority, the cold-blooded counsels of commonsense.

It was to me the remotest of chances that I should ever be driven to weigh, as they did, the value of a sentence, a word, or a look : and yet, now, not three months after I had left Canada, this was precisely what I found myself doing.

I knew, as I awoke, the morning after Nugent's visit, that some strange and delightful thing had befallen me ; but I waited in dreamy security, till the tremor of happiness stirred me to a clearer knowledge of itself. Slowly it all came back to me. In imagination I lived again through what had happened yesterday. The long afternoon of waiting, the tension of the trivial talk, thinly interposed between two hearts that every instant brought nearer to one another ; the uncertainty as to his meaning ; and then—I put my hand over my eyes, dizzy even at the remembrance—the certainty that he loved me.

Looking back over the time I had known him, I could not understand how this improbable, this incredible thing had come about. Until the night of the Jackson-Crolys' dance I had never admitted to myself that I did more than like his society, and till then I had had still less idea that he did more than care for mine.

With a shamefaced smile at my own foolishness, I got out my diary, and searched through it for some mention of Nugent on the days on which I remembered to have met him. But its bald and unimaginative record had chronicled no description of him beyond one pithy entry after the first day's hunting :—

" Mr. O'Neill piloted me. Dull and conceited."

I remember quite well the satisfaction with which I had permitted myself this brilliant analysis of character : and I laughed outright as I thought how the girl who had written that would have despised her future self if she could have foreseen in what spirit it would again be referred to.

I slowly thought over the various stages of our

acquaintance, ending, as I had begun, with the events of yesterday, and that unanswered question of his. Well, I should certainly see him to-morrow ; perhaps even to-day, I thought, and trembled at the thought.

When I went down to breakfast I found that Willy had finished his. This was practically our first *tête-à-tête* since he had come home. Last night he had not come into the drawing-room after dinner, and I had gone to my room early. He was standing in the window, reading a letter, when I came into the room, and, with a keen dart of memory, my first morning at Durrus came into my mind. He had been standing in just that position as I came in to breakfast that first morning after my arrival, and I well remembered the smile with which he had come forward to meet me. The contrast of his present greeting jarred painfully on me, and dashed a little the serenity in which I had tried to enwrap myself. The old boyish friendliness was all gone, and in its place was a spasmodic, constrained politeness, which was so foreign to his nature, and so hardly assumed, that it seemed to me the most pitiful thing in the world. I came near wishing that I had never seen Nugent, and I thought with humiliation of what Willy would feel when he knew how much my denials about him had been worth.

" I breakfasted earlier to-day," he said awkwardly. " I have to be in Esker at eleven o'clock. Is there anything I can do for you there ? "

" No, thank you. But, Willy "—as he was leaving the room—" that reminds me, the O'Neills want me

to ride with them to Mount Prospect to-morrow.
Could I have Blackthorn ? "

" Of course you can," he answered gruffly ; " you
know you've only to order the horse when you want
him."

" Would you come with us ? " I went on timidly.

" No, thanks ; I'm very busy about the farm just
now."

He opened the door and went away.

I had no heart to eat any breakfast. All the glad-
ness of the morning had died ; but it had struck deep,
and by its preciousness it had taught me once and for
ever what suffering might mean. I was still daw-
dling over my teacup when Roche came in to clear
away the breakfast things. His professional eye at
once detected my unused plate.

" Will I get another egg biled for you, miss ?
Them's cold."

" No, thank you, Roche. I'm not very hungry
this morning."

Roche turned a shrewd eye, like a parrot's, upon
me.

" Fie, fie, miss ! That's no way for a young lady
to be. And Masther Willy wasn't much better than
yourself. You have a right to be out this fine morning, and not sitting that way over the fire."

As much to escape from Roche's acute and sympathetic observation as for any other reason, I left the
dining-room, and wandered aimlessly into the hall.

Whinings and scratchings outside the door decided me to try what the day felt like. I wrapped a

carriage rug round my shoulders, and, putting on the cap which Willy had once made over to me, I opened the hall door, and was at once assaulted by Pat and Jinny. Having exhausted themselves in ambitious attempts to lick my face by means of perpendicular leaps at it, they proceeded to explain to me their wish that I should take them to the garden, to hunt, for the hundredth time, a rabbit which had long set at naught the best-laid plots for his destruction. I followed them to the old gate—a structure in itself very characteristic of Durrus—and opened it in the usual way, by kicking away a stone that had been placed against it, and by then putting my hand through a hole to reach the latch, whose catch on the outside had been broken.

I did not feel disposed to-day to help Pat and Jinny in their hunt, by struggling, as Willy and I had so often done, through the rows of big wet cabbages, whose crinkled white hearts showed the devastations of the enemy, and, leaving the dogs to form their own plan of campaign, I sauntered up and down the path between the lichen-crusted gooseberry-trees. In spite of Roche's recommendation of the weather, I thought it a very cheerless morning. There was a bite in the chilly air, and each time I turned at the end of the walk and faced the gate, the breeze that met me was sharp and raw.

It was early in January—the deadest time of all the year, I thought, looking round. Not a sign of spring, no feeling even of the hope of it ; and somehow, in this cold, leaden atmosphere, my own happiness began to lose some of its radiance. I turned and once more walked towards the gate, thinking that I would call the dogs from their futile yelpings at the mouth of the hole to which the rabbit had long since betaken himself, and would go for a walk. I was not more than half-way down the path, when I saw a hand put through the hole in the gate. As it felt for the latch, I quickly recognised its lean pallor; the gate opened, and Uncle Dominick came into the garden.

"Good-morning, my dear," he said. "I thought I saw you going into this wilderness of ours that we call a kitchen garden, and I followed you in the hopes of having a little chat."

He was evidently in the best of humours—nothing else could have accounted for this unwonted desire for society, and, in spite of the dark rings under his eyes and the yellow sodden look of his skin, he looked unusually benign and cheerful.

"Perhaps you will take a turn with me round the garden," he continued affably. "I can see you are not dressed for a longer walk; although I do not for a moment wish to disparage your costume. Indeed, I do not know that I have ever seen you wear anything that becomes you more than that cap of Willy's!"

I turned with him, and we walked slowly round the grass-grown paths which followed the square of the walls, stooping every now and then to save our eyes from the unpruned boughs of the apple-trees.

"Dear me! this place is shockingly neglected,"

my uncle said, twitching a bramble out of my way with his stick; "in old days it was a very different affair. My mother used to have four men at work here, and I remember well when it was the best garden in the country."

We had by this time come to the dilapidated old hothouse, and we both stood and looked at it for a few seconds. Through the innumerable broken panes, and under the decaying window-sashes, the branches of a peach-tree thrust themselves out in every direction, as if breaking loose from imprisonment.

"Ah, the poor old peach-house!" said Uncle Dominick, digging a weed out of the path with the heel of his boot—"that was another of my mother's hobbies. I wish I had the energy and the money to get this whole place put to rights," he continued, as we walked on again; "but I have neither the one nor the other. I shall leave all that for Willy to do some day; for he is fond of the old place. Do you not think so, my dear?"

"I am sure he is," I answered, rather absently; my thoughts had strayed away to to-morrow's ride.

"I suppose you have seen Willy this morning? Did he seem in better spirits than he was in last night? I don't know that I ever saw him so depressed and silent as he was at dinner," said my uncle.

"Did you think so?" I replied guiltily. "I think he seemed all right this morning."

"I am very glad to hear it. I was quite distressed

by his manner ; indeed, latterly I have frequently noticed how variable his spirits have been."

I did not speak, and Uncle Dominick went on again with a little hesitation—

" I will confess to you, my dear Theo, that before you came Willy had been causing me very serious anxiety. You see, this is a lonely place ; the O'Neills are much away from home, and he had no companions of his own age and station."

" No, I suppose not," I said, considerably puzzled as to the drift of all this.

My uncle stroked his long moustache several times.

" Well, my dear, you know the old proverb, ' No company, welcome trumpery ' ; that, I am sorry to say, is what the danger was with Willy. It came to my knowledge that he was in the habit of—a—of spending a great deal of his time in the house of—" he hummed and hawed, ending with suppressed vehemence—" in the house of one of my work-people."

I held my breath, with perhaps some presentiment of what was coming.

" Yes," my uncle said, bringing his stick heavily down on the ground ; " I heard, to my amazement and horror, that the attraction for him there was the daughter, an impudent girl, who was evidently using every means in her power to entangle him ! "

" An impudent girl ! " What was it that he had once said about a girl who had been taken out of her proper place, and had at once begun to presume ?

In the same instant the answer flashed upon me—
Anstey! Of course, it was she. How had I been
so blind?

My uncle was silent for a few moments, and my
thoughts raced back to incidents, unconsidered at
the time, but now fraught with a new meaning. I
understood it all now—the girl standing in the niche
at the lodge gate; the words which I had overheard
at the plantation; the figure in the rain at the hall
door on the night of the dance, and Michael Brian's
threats after the bonfire.

"I was delighted to see, after you came, what an
influence for good you at once seemed to exert over
him," Uncle Dominick began again. "I cannot say
how grateful to you I have felt. The thought that
Willy might be led on into doing anything to lower
the family preyed upon me more than I can tell you,
and it gave me the greatest pleasure to see what his
feelings for you were."

What could I say? Horror at this revelation,
pity for Anstey, bitter, sick disappointment in Willy,
together with the knowledge of what my uncle so
obviously expected of me, were pursuing each other
through my mind.

"I feared, from his behaviour last night, that there
had occurred some misunderstanding between you."
He stood still, and looked at me interrogatively.
"Of course, I do not ask for your confidence in the
matter, but I think you know as well as I do what
effect anything serious of that kind would have on
him."

Honesty compelled me to speak. "I ought to have told you before," I began falteringly, "that I was thinking—I had almost settled that I was going back to Canada."

"To Canada? Impossible!" he exclaimed, in a startled but dictatorial voice; then, forcing a laugh, "Of course, I know you are a very independent young lady, but I have belief enough in you to think that you would not desert your friends."

"I cannot do what you want me to," I said incoherently; "I should be staying here on false pretences. I must go away."

"Nonsense!" he said impatiently. "I beg your pardon, my dear, but your ideas of duty appear to me a little peculiar. I think, *all things considered*, you could scarcely reconcile it—I will not say with your conscience, but with your sense of honour—to let Willy ruin his whole life without stretching out a hand to stop him."

"But I don't know what you mean. You know I would do almost anything for Willy; but why should I be bound by my 'sense of honour' to stay here?"

I spoke stoutly, but in my inmost soul I dreaded his answer.

"Well," said my uncle, with a disagreeable expression, "I think that most people would agree with me, that a young lady is bound in honour not to give such encouragement to a man as will raise hopes that she does not mean to gratify."

There was truth enough in what he said to make

me feel a difficulty in replying. We had come to the gate, and he opened it for me.

" I do not wish to press you on this subject, my dear, but I am sure that, after you have thought it over a little, your fairness, as well as your kind heart, will make you feel the truth of what I have been saying to you."

That was all he said, but it was enough. I went back to the house, feeling that, whatever happened, trouble was before me.

Roche met me on the steps with a note on a salver. I knew the handwriting, and opened it with a pulse quickened by a delightful glow of confidence and expectancy. I read it through twice over ; then, mechanically replacing it in the envelope, I went up to my own room, and throwing myself on my bed, I pressed my face into the pillow and wished that I were dead.

CHAPTER XXIV.

THE fire in the library was dying out. I had been sitting on the hearthrug in front of it for some time, with my elbows resting on the seat of a low arm-chair, from whose depths Jinny's snores rose with quiet regularity. The window had been grey with the last of the dull light when I first sat down there, and, without stirring, I had watched the grey fading by imperceptible changes from mere blankness into an absolute darkness, that invaded the room and filled it like a cloud.

The turf fire, with soft noises of subsidence, had sunk lower and lower in the grate, and, abandoning its effort to light up the heavy lines of bookshelves, now did little more than edge with a feeble glow the shadow of the chimney-piece upon the ceiling. A few minutes before, a flicker had leaped up from the red embers; it had not lasted long, but the transient glare had made my eyes ache. For two or three seconds afterwards the blackened fragments of a sheet of notepaper had been shaken and lifted uncertainly by the thin turf smoke, and they were now drifting away with it up the chimney. My hand, lying open upon my knee, still retained the sensation of holding something which had been clasped tightly in it all the afternoon—the letter which I had just burnt—and it seemed to me that in my heart there was the same sense of emptiness and loss.

It had cost me something to burn it, and as the flame crept over the pages, I had come near snatching it back again. But after all there was no need to keep it ; its contents were not so long nor so intricate, I thought bitterly, that there was any fear of my forgetting them.

" DEAR MISS SARSFIELD " (it began),

" My sister has asked me to tell you that she has been obliged to change her plans, and is leaving Clashmore to-morrow instead of next week. She desires me to say how sorry she is at having to give up the ride to Mount Prospect, and to go away without seeing you. She would write herself, but is too much hurried. I fear that I must make the same apologies on my own account, as I find that I shall have to go to London in a few days, and may possibly not return before the summer ; and, as I am afraid I shall not be able to get over to Durrus, perhaps you will kindly let me say good-bye by letter.

" Sincerely yours,

" NUGENT O'NEILL."

Nothing could have been more simply put ; nothing could have expressed more incisively the writer's meaning. Even in the first moment of reading it, I had been at no loss to understand it.

He had gone a little farther than he had intended, and he now lost no time in removing any undue impression that his words might have made upon me. What was it that Willy had told me long ago—how long ago ?—of the " musical flirtation with the Yankee girl at Cannes ! "

Possibly he would now be able to add another " queer story " to his record—how, in the course of a most ordinary flirtation, he had discovered one afternoon that the girl was losing her head, and how he had been obliged to leave the country so as to avoid further difficulties.

The last scrap of the letter fluttered upwards out of sight as this idea, which it had suggested, came into my mind. The intolerable sting of the thought acted on me like physical pain. I started up, but by the time I was on my feet I was ashamed of it. " No," I said to myself vehemently, " he would never do that ; I have no right even to think it of him. He *was* in earnest when he was speaking to me ; I know it ! Perhaps *he* lost his head too, and then when he got home he thought better of it, and felt it was only fair to let me understand as soon as possible that he meant nothing serious. Why was I a fool— an utter fool ? " I asked myself desperately. " Whatever he meant, I had better begin at once, as he has done, to forget it all," I thought, as I groped my way out of the room ; " but just now I feel as if it would take me all my life."

As I dressed for dinner, I shrank from the prospect of the long difficult hours that lay between me and the solitude of my own room. But I think that my powers of further suffering must have been exhausted; a benumbing weariness was my only sensation as I sat at the dinner-table, and, looking from my uncle to my cousin, felt, in some far-off way, that our lives were converging to their point of closest contact, perhaps to their climax of mutual suffering.

I had not energy to talk, and I occupied myself for the most part in efforts to keep up the semblance of eating my dinner. Willy went on with his in a kind of resigned surliness, taking as little notice of me as was compatible with common politeness. This state of things I should much have preferred to any open signs of enmity or friendship, if I had not noticed that my uncle was narrowly observing us, and was even making various attempts to involve us both in the conversation, which had hitherto been little more than a monologue upon his part. Beyond an occasional grunt, Willy did not even try to respond ; and as for me, though I did my best, utter mental and bodily fatigue made the framing of a sentence too laborious for me.

Several times during the progress of dinner, I found that Roche was looking at me with anxious interest ; and once or twice he came to my rescue by quietly changing my plate as quickly as possible, so that my uncle should not see how little I had eaten of what he had sent me.

Dinner was longer, and Uncle Dominick more determinately talkative, than usual ; but at last there came a break in his harangue, and I took advantage of it to make my escape into the drawing-room. I sat for a long time over the fire by myself, lying in an arm-chair without any wish to move. I felt as if I had sunk to the bottom of a deep sea, whose waves were rushing and surging over my head, and I wondered dully if this was what people felt like when they were going to have a bad illness. My mind kept stupidly repeating one short sentence, " Let me say good-bye ! Let me say good-bye ! " They were the last words I had seen of Nugent's letter as it curled up in the flame of the library fire, and they now beat to and fro in my brain with sing-song monotony.

I believe I must have dozed, for the noise of the door opening aroused me with a shivering start. Willy came into the room with a newspaper in his hand, and, sitting down at the other side of the fire without speaking to me, began to read it. I fell back in my chair again, waiting till the striking of ten o'clock should give me a reasonable excuse for going to bed. The crackling of Willy's newspaper and the sleepy tick of the clock were the only sounds in the room. I had never before seen Willy read a newspaper so attentively, and I watched him with languid interest from under my half-closed eyelids, while he steadily made his way through it. Now he had turned it inside out, and was reading the advertisements ; certainly it did not take much to amuse him. Could he have felt, on that day after the dance, as dead to all the things that used to interest him as I did now ?

Here I found myself face to face with the problem that has tortured many women. How could Willy be in love with me, with any sincerity—and yet I could not doubt his sincerity—when only a month before he had, by his own admission, been in love with a country girl? It could not torture me, but I was young and enthusiastic, and it cut at the heart of my belief in human nature.

It was only four evenings ago since I had listened miserably to the passionate words that I had not been able to prevent him from saying; he must have forgotten them already, or how else could he sit there with such stolid composure? If he could recover his equanimity in four days, perhaps in a week I should have begun to forget that persistent sentence which still kept pace with my thoughts.

The dining-room door opened and shut with a loud bang, and I heard the sound of uncertain footsteps crossing the hall. The crackling of the newspaper ceased, and a sudden rigidity in Willy's attitude showed me that he was listening. The step paused outside the door, and then, after some preliminary rattling, the handle was turned. Willy jumped up and walked quickly to the door, as if with the intention of stopping whoever was there from coming in. Before he reached it, however, it opened, and I saw that it was his father whose entrance he had been trying to prevent.

"It's not worth while your coming in, sir," he said; "Theo's awfully tired, and she's going to bed."

"Tired! what right has she to be tired?" said my

uncle, loudly, coming into the room as he spoke. He put his hand on Willy's shoulder and pushed him to one side. " Get out of my way ! Why should I not come in if I like ? "

He walked very slowly and deliberately to the fireplace, and stood on the rug with his back to the fire, swinging a little backwards and forwards from his toes to his heels. There was some difference in his manner and appearance which I could not account for. His face was ghastly white ; a scant lock of iron-grey hair hung over his forehead ; and the dark rings I had seen about his eyes in the morning had now changed to a purplish red.

" And what have you two been doing with yourselves all the evening ? Making the most of your time, Willy, I hope ? Perhaps that was why you tried to keep me out just now ? "

He began to laugh at what he had said in a way very unusual with him.

" Theo," Willy said abruptly, interrupting his father's laughter, " you're looking dead beat ; I'll go and light your candle."

" What are you in such a hurry about ? " demanded Uncle Dominick, turning on Willy with unexpected fierceness. " Don't you know it is manners to wait till you're asked ? "

Willy did not answer, but went out into the hall ; and I, feeling both scared and angry, got up with the intention of following him as quickly as possible.

" Good-night, Uncle Dominick," I said icily.

He bent forward and took hold of my arm, leaning his whole weight upon it.

" Look here," he whispered confidentially ; " how has that fellow been behaving ? You haven't forgotten our little talk this morning, eh ? "

" I remember it quite well. Good-night," I repeated, trying to pull my arm from his detaining hand, and move away.

The action nearly threw him off his balance ; he gave a stagger, and was in the act of recovering himself by the help of my arm, when Willy came back with the lighted candle.

" For goodness' sake, let her go to bed," he said, striding over to where we were standing, and looking threateningly at his father.

Uncle Dominick dropped my arm. " What the devil do you mean by interfering with me, sir ? " he said. " Let me tell you that I will not stand this behaviour on your part any longer ! I suppose you think you can treat your cousin and me as if we were no better than your low companions ? I know where you spent your afternoon to-day. I know what those infernal people are plotting and scheming for. But I can tell you, that if they can make a fool of you they shall not make one of me ! This house is mine. And you may tell them from me, that as sure as I am standing here "—emphasising each word with a trembling hand, while he clutched the mantel-shelf with the other—" you shall never set foot in it, or touch one penny of my money, if——"

" Look here ! " said Willy, stepping forward be-

tween me and his father, " that's enough ; you'd
better shut up."

" How dare you speak to me like that ? Your con-
duct is not that of a gentleman, sir !—not that of a
gentleman ! I say, sir, it is not—that—of——" His
voice had grown thicker and more unsteady at every
word.

" Here's your candle," said Willy, thrusting the
candlestick into my hand ; " you'd better go."

" She shall not be ordered about by you ! " thun-
dered my uncle, making an ineffectual step or two to
stop me. " She shall stay here as long as I like. I
will be master in my own house. Come back here ! "

He spoke with such fury that I was afraid to go,
and looked irresolutely to Willy for help. But before he could speak, my uncle's mood had changed.

" Let her go if she likes," he said suddenly, staring
at me with a sort of stupefaction. " Good God ! Let
her go if she likes ; let her go ! " he cried, covering
his eyes with his hands and dropping into a chair.

CHAPTER XXV.

I DO not often get a headache, but the one which woke me next morning seemed determined to bring my average of pain up to the level of that of less fortunate people. All day long it pressed like a burning cap over my head, till my pillow felt as if it were a block of wood, and the thin chinks of light that came through the closed shutters cut my eyes like the blades of knives. The infrequent sounds in the quiet house—the far-off shutting of a door, the knocking of the housemaid's broom against the wainscot in the corridor, or an occasional footstep in the hall—all jarred upon my aching brain as if it had lost some accustomed shelter, and the blows of sound struck directly upon its bruised nerves.

The wretchedness of the day before had given way to the supremacy of physical suffering. I lay in my darkened room, thinking of nothing except how best to endure the passing of the slow hours. Once, as the clock in the hall struck three, I was conscious of some association connected with the sound, and remembered that this was the hour at which I should have been starting for Mount Prospect.

But it had all lost reality. Even the horror of that scene with my uncle and Willy in the drawing-room had been for the time obliterated, wiped out by the pain of which it had partly been the cause. All that I felt was that some trouble surely was there, and, though in abeyance for to-day, it was already in possession of to-morrow, and of many to-morrows.

When, on the next morning, after breakfast in bed, I made my way downstairs, I felt as if a long time had gone by since I had crossed the hall. The house was cold and deserted. I dreaded meeting my uncle, but I saw no one; there was not even a dog to wish me good-morning. In the drawing-room, the fire had only just been lighted; the blinds were drawn to the top of the windows, showing the various layers of dust in the room, from the venerable accumulation under the piano, to the lighter and more recent coating on the tables. I went straight to the writing-table, and, regardless of the cheerless glare from the sheet of grey sea, I began a letter to Aunt Margaret.

Upstairs, in the early hours of the morning, it had seemed an easy and not disagreeable thing to do—to write and tell her that my Irish visit was over, and that, as soon as her answer had come, I should be glad to go back to Canada. But when the letter was closed and directed, I sat looking at it for a long time, feeling that I had done something akin to making my will. The best part of my life was over; into these past three months had been crushed its keenest happiness and unhappiness, and this was what they had amounted to. They had none the less now to fall into the background, and soon would have no more connection with my future life than if they had never been.

I had convinced myself so thoroughly that by writing to Aunt Margaret I had closed this epoch in my life, that when, a few minutes afterwards, Willy came into the room, I was almost surprised to find that he was as awkward and constrained as when I had seen him last.

"Oh! I didn't know you were in here, Theo," he said apologetically, stopping short half-way across the room. "I only came in to look for a pen." He rolled his cap in his hands and looked at the ground.

"I hope your head's all right to-day? The governor was asking after you yesterday. He was very sorry to hear your headache was so bad."

I knew that he was trying, as well as he could, to apologise for his father's outbreak and its too obvious cause.

"That was very kind of him," I said quickly. "My headache is quite well. I was thinking of going out, as it looks as if the east wind had gone."

"Yes, it's a nice day. I dare say it would do you good to go out."

Nothing could have made me feel more plainly the break that had come in what had been such "a fair fellowship" than his making no offer to come with me, and I realised with sharp regret that I had done well in writing that letter to Aunt Margaret.

Willy turned to leave the room.

"I wanted to tell you about this letter," I said. "I have just written to Aunt Margaret to say that I am going back to Canada in about a fortnight."

His back had been towards me when I began to speak, but he faced round with an exclamation of astonishment.

"What! going away? Why are you doing that?"

His face was red with surprise, and he had forgotten his shyness.

"I thought Uncle Dominick would have told you. I spoke to him a couple of days ago."

"He never said so to me. On the contrary——" Willy stopped. "I mean, he didn't give me the least idea you were going."

"For all that, I am afraid I must go. I have been here an immense time already," I said, finding some difficulty in maintaining an easy and conventional tone.

"Indeed, you haven't!" he blurted out. "You know you told me you meant to stay on into the spring, and——and you know"——looking steadily over my head out of the window while he spoke——"there's no reason why——"

"Oh yes, there is," I said, interrupting him. "Aunt Margaret wants help with all those children. I ought not to leave her alone any more."

"Well, and won't you be leaving us alone too?"—— still without changing the direction of his eyes.

"Oh! you will be no worse off than you were

before I came," I answered, with the hasty indiscretion of argument, and not without a biting thought of Anstey Brian.

He did not reply, and I had time to be sorry, before he said, with an assumption of carelessness :—

"Well, I'm going out now, and I advise you to do the same." He left the room ; but, reopening the door, put his head in—"I say, don't send that letter," he said, and shut the door again before I could answer.

I did not meet Uncle Dominick at lunch. Roche told me not to wait for him, as he was not well, and would probably not come in ; and I had almost finished my solitary meal before Willy appeared. He and I were both more at our ease than we had been at our first meeting that morning. I do not know what had operated in his case, but for myself, I felt more than ever that I had become a different person—a person to whom nothing mattered very much, whose only link with the everyday life of the past and present was a very bitter and humiliating pain.

"I have to go into Esker this afternoon," said Willy, occupying himself very busily with the carving of the cold beef. "I was wondering if you might care to ride there. The horse wants exercise, and I thought perhaps—you said something about wanting fresh air——"

I did not know how to refuse an invitation so humbly given, although my first inclination had been to do so.

" It is rather a long ride," I began doubtfully.

" Well, you can turn back whenever you like."

I debated with myself. As I was going away so soon, it could not make much real difference to any one ; and Uncle Dominick had specially asked me not to neglect Willy. Besides—I could not help it —some faint hope struggled up in my heart that in Esker I might hear something of the O'Neills.

" Very well," I said finally, " I will go with you."

Willy and I had often ridden to Esker. It was a long ride, and we had established a short cut across the fields, though experience had shown us that the amount of jumping it involved, and the rough ground to be crossed, did away with any great saving of time. To-day we went in off the road at the usual gap, and as we cantered over the grass to the accustomed spot in each fence, the free stride of the horse, and the tingling of the wind in my cheeks, brought back the old feeling of exultant independence, the last remnant of my headache cleared away, and for the time I even forgot that quiet, incessant aching at my heart.

One or two successful conflicts with his horse had done much to restore Willy's confidence and self-possession.

" It's a long time since we had a ride now," he said, after we had come out over a bank on to the road again.

" Yes ; I was just thinking the same. I am very glad I came out."

" We must try and get a look at the hounds next week ; they meet pretty close—that is to say "—

continuing his sentence with something of a jerk—
" if you're not too busy packing then."

I did not answer, and Willy said nothing more
until we had pulled up into a walk on some rising
ground, from which we could see the town of Esker
straggling out of an opening between two hills, its
whitewashed houses showing dimly through the blue
smoke that lay about it like a lake.

" And did you send that letter, after all ? " Willy
said in an unconcerned way.

" Yes," I answered ; " you know I always write to
Canada on Friday."

" Then you mean to say you are really going
back ? "

I nodded.

" Well, I suppose you know best," he said coldly.

Alaska put her foot on a stone, and stumbled
slightly.

" Hold up, you confounded fool ! " he said chuck-
ing up her head roughly, and digging his spurs in.

The mare reared and plunged, and to steady her
we broke into a trot, which brought us into the
crooked, crowded streets of Esker.

It was market-day, and the carts that had come in
with their loads of butter, turf, fowls and old women
blocked our way in every direction. I remained on
my horse's back while Willy went off about his
business, and for the next half-hour I only caught
glimpses of him, doubling round the immovable
groups of talkers, and eluding the beggars with
practised skill as he dived in and out of the little

shops. Willy's satisfaction and confidence in the warehouses of Esker, and the amount of shopping which he contrived to do there, had always been a matter of fresh surprise to me.

Beggars pestered me ; little boys exasperated me by offers to hold Blackthorn, regardless of the fact that I was on his back ; and women clustered round me on the pavement and discussed my lineage and appearance, but I was too dispirited to be much amused by their comments. The glow of my gallop had faded out ; I felt cold and tired, and thought that Willy had never before been so long over his shopping.

At last he appeared unexpectedly at my horse's shoulder.

" I was thinking that you must be dead for want of tea. I've just ordered some at Reardon's, and you must come and have it before we go home."

I assented without much interest, and began to push Blackthorn through the crowd. At the hotel I dismounted, and followed Willy listlessly into the dark, unsavoury commercial room. Its sole occupant got up in obedience to a whisper from the boots, and hurriedly conveyed himself and his glass of whisky and water from the room which had been allotted to him and the gentlemen of his profession, and I sat down at the long oilcloth-covered table and began to pour out the tea, while Willy battered the fire into a blaze. He had evidently made up his mind to be cheerful, but as evidently he was not quite certain as to what to talk about.

I listened with as much intelligence as I could

muster to such pieces of news as he had picked up during his shopping, but our conversation gradually slackened, and finally came to a full stop. I slowly drank the contents of my enormous teacup, wondering why it was that at country hotels the bread and butter and the china were alike abnormally thick. I noticed that Willy had looked at me undecidedly once or twice during the last few minutes, and at length he said, in a way that showed he had been framing the question for some time—

" I suppose, if you went away, you'd be coming back again ? "

" Come back ! " I echoed. " No, I do not think there is the least chance of my doing that."

I had finished my tea, and got up as I spoke.

" Then you've done with this country altogether ? "

" Yes ; altogether," I answered resolutely, turning aside to study one of the oleographs on the walls.

I could not have said another word, and, in a sort of defiance of my own weakness, I began to hum a tune, one that had been in my mind unrecognised all day. Now as I hummed it the straining sweetness of the notes of a violin filled my memory, and I knew where and how I had heard it last.

Willy said nothing more, and, getting up, rang the bell and ordered the horses to be brought round. We had to stand for a minute in the doorway while they were coming. A cold wind was springing up with the sunset ; the pale yellow light was contending with the newly lighted street-lamps, and over my head a large jet of gas flickered drearily behind the name " Reardon " on the fanlight.

"Hullo! look at the Clashmore waggonette," Willy said suddenly. " It's coming along now behind that string of turf-carts. I suppose they're going to the station."

The turf-carts lumbered slowly to a full stop, and the chestnuts and waggonette had perforce to pull up opposite the hotel. On the box, sharply outlined against the frosty sky, I saw Nugent's figure, and inside was a huddled mass of furs, which I supposed was Madam O'Neill. My first instinct was to shrink back into the hall, but it was too late ; Willy was already taking off his hat, and I bowed mechanically as Nugent lifted his.

" You're off to-night, I suppose ? " Willy called out ; " will you be away long ? "

" Yes, I dare say I shall not be home for some time, I'm thinking of going abroad for a bit."

" Abroad ? Where to ? Is it to Cannes again ? "

" Quite possibly," said Nugent.

The turf-carts moved on, and the chestnuts pranced impatiently.

" Good-bye," said Nugent, in a voice as chill as the frosty air of the evening. He lifted his hat, and the carriage was gone.

We rode quickly and steadily homewards through the darkening hills, without a word to break the silence between us. I had no wish to speak, no wish for anything but to escape from this miserable place and to forget all that had happened to me since the night when I had first driven along this very road. This was the fulfilment of the insane unacknowledged hope which had been my real reason for to-day's ride. I had met Nugent, and could take home with me the certainty that I had made no mistake as to what his letter had meant, and that he, for his part, would be quite sure that having failed with him, I was now consoling myself with my cousin.

It was quite dark when we got to Durrus, but, as the gates swung back, I could see that it was Anstey who had opened them for us. I rode through a little in advance of Willy, who had checked his horse in order to let me go first. I thought I caught the sound of a whispered word or two from Anstey, and, with the clang of the closing gate, I distinctly heard Willy say in a low voice, " No, I can't."

I rode fast up the avenue so that he should not overtake me. Here, had it been needed, was further confirmation of what my uncle had told me. Everything was going wrong. I had spoilt my own life, and now I had to stand by and see Willy ruin his, knowing that I had it, perhaps, in my power to save him, and yet feeling incapable of doing so.

When I met Uncle Dominick at dinner, his manner was more blandly affectionate than I had ever known it, and but for the recollections which his haggard face called up, I should have thought that the scene of two nights ago had been a dream.

CHAPTER XXVI.

I LAY awake for a long time after I got into bed, and I had not been long asleep when some sound wakened me. I was at first not sorry to awake ; I had been sleeping uneasily and feverishly, and my dreams had been full of disasters and difficulties. I did not trouble myself much as to what the sound was— probably a rat, as the house was overrun with them —and I tried to see the face of my watch by the light of the fire, which was still burning brightly. I had made out that it was half-past one, when I again heard a sound. It was a movement in the next room, as if a chair had been pushed against by some one moving cautiously in the dark. I do not pretend to being superior to irrational terrors at night, and now the blood rushed back to my head from my heart, as I sat up in bed and tried to per-suade myself that what I had heard was the effect of imagination.

There was dead silence for a few seconds, and then a hand was passed over the other side of the paper-covered door, as if feeling for the latch.

I have had some bad moments in my life, but I have known nothing much worse than the possibilities of those seconds while the invisible hand groped for the latch. The door was weak and badly fitting, made of single planks, and it at first refused to open, but it had finally to yield to the pressure applied to it. It opened with a jerk, and I saw by the firelight that the figure which appeared in the doorway was neither ghost nor burglar ; it was Anstey Brian's mother.

" What do you want ? " I demanded, as firmly as I could.

She stood still and looked at me. The firelight flickered on her face, I saw her lips moving incessantly, but no sound came from them. With a tremendous effort I broke through the cold trance of terror, and said loudly, " If you don't go away at once, I shall call the master ! "

At this, to my unspeakable relief, she looked hastily over her shoulder, and drawing the hood of her cloak over her head, she retreated into the room from which she had come, closing the paper-covered door after her.

I listened intently, and presently heard the rustle of her cloak against the walls as she went down the corridor, and soon afterwards a door at some distant part of the house opened and shut.

I drew a long breath ; she was out of the house now. I got up, and, with shaking limbs, dragged my big trunk against the paper-covered door, and, having locked the other one, felt comparatively secure.

But my heart alternately thumped and fluttered against my side ; fright, combined with indignation with Willy, with Uncle Dominick, and chiefly with the Brians and their inveteracy as disturbers of the peace of Durrus, kept me awake till morning, seething with a resolve to escape as soon as possible from this disastrous household.

At breakfast I told Willy what had happened. He was out of spirits, and not like himself, and I had put off saying anything to him about it until we had almost finished breakfast. When I had ended my story, he pushed back his chair from the table and got up.

" I'll make them sorry for this," he said vindictively, his face flushing darkly as he spoke. " I'll teach that old scoundrel Brian to let Moll come up here frightening you ! You look as white as a sheet this minute."

" I am sure I am nothing of the kind," I answered, trying unsuccessfully to look at myself in the silver teapot ; " there is nothing the matter with me. If you will fasten up that little door into the other room before this evening, I shall be perfectly happy."

" Never fear but I will," he said ; " and it'll be very queer if I don't fasten up that old hag too."

He stalked out of the room. I heard him go upstairs and along the corridor, and presently the noise of hammering echoed through the house.

I met him in the hall soon afterwards, putting on his cap to go out.

" I fixed that door the way it won't be opened again in a hurry," he said, with grim satisfaction, " and I've locked the other. Here's the key for you. Now I'm going to be off to fix Moll herself. She's not such a fool but she'll understand what I'm going to say to her ! "

" I wonder what the attraction in that room was for her ? " I said. " I have seen her in there several times."

" Goodness knows ! There was nothing in it, only an old broken chair she had by the window, and there were a couple of books on the floor that I suppose she stole out of the study to play with. One looked like an old diary, or account-book, or something. I meant to bring them out of it, but I forgot them."

" I am very much obliged to you for shutting up that door," I said, with sincere gratitude. " I had no idea you were going to do it for me at once. You are a most reliable person."

He had taken his stick out of the stand, and had opened the hall door ; but he stopped and looked back at me.

" I think I'd do more than that for you," he said, almost under his breath, and went out of the house.

It was a fine morning, and I finally went for a walk along the cliffs with the dogs. I expected to hear all about Willy's encounter with Moll at luncheon ;

but, on my return to the house, I heard, to my surprise, that he had driven into Esker, with his portmanteau, to catch the train for Cork, and would not be home till the following evening.

The afternoon lagged by. I had tea early, in the hope of shortening it ; but the device did not have much success. As the evening clouded in, rain began to beat in large drops against the windows, and the rising wind sighed about the house, and sent puffs of smoke down the drawing-room chimney. I despised myself for the feeling of forsakenness which it gave me ; but I could help it no more than I could hinder some apprehensive recollections of Moll's entry into my room. A childish dread of having all the darkness behind me made me crouch down on the hearthrug, with my back to the fire, and rouse Pat from a satiated slumber to sit on my lap for company. Something about the look of the fire and the sound of the rain was compelling my thoughts back to the afternoon when I sat and waited here for Nugent. I did not try, as I had so often tried before, to drive away those thoughts, or to forget the withheld possibilities of that afternoon. Once more I gave myself over to the fascination of unprofitable remembrances, yielding to myself on the plea that it was to be for the last time. After to-day they would be contraband, made outlaws by the power of a resolution which I had newly come to—a resolution that I had been driven to by the combined forces of pity and sympathy and conscience ; but to-day, for one final half-hour, I would allow them to have their way.

Dinner-time came, and with it no appearance of Willy. Uncle Dominick had for some time given up his custom of waiting in the library to take me in to dinner, and Willy and I usually found him sitting by the fire in the dining-room when we went in. To-night, however, he was not there.

"The master's not coming in to dinner; he's not well at all, miss," said Roche mysteriously. "I was telling him a while ago that 'tis for the docthor he should send; but indeed, he was for turning me out of the room when I said it."

"Do you think he would like to see me?"

"Don't go near him at all to-night, miss," Roche answered, with unexpected urgency. "He'll be betther to-morrow—you'll see him then."

But I did see my uncle again that night. When I went upstairs to bed, I was startled by seeing his tall figure, in his dressing-gown, standing outside the door of the room which Willy had locked. He had a large bunch of keys, and was trying them one after the other in the lock.

"Perhaps you can help me with these," he said, looking round as I came up to him. "I am almost sure that one of these keys opens this door, but I cannot find it."

His hand trembled so much, that the keys were shaking and jingling as he held them out to me.

"I am afraid the key is not on this bunch——" I began.

"But, my dear, I think it is very probable that we shall find Willy in that room," he said in a low confidential voice, pressing the keys upon me. " I cannot think why he remains in there. I have tried several times to-day to open the door, but that fellow Roche keeps pestering me. I believe he is in league with Willy."

My own hand was trembling almost as much as my uncle's, but I did not dare to refuse to take the keys, and I made a pretence of trying one in the lock. He watched me anxiously for a moment.

" No, my dear, I see it is no use trying to-night. You are tired, and so am I "—he sighed deeply, and put his hand to his chest,—" this oppression that I am suffering from tries me terribly. I will go to my room and see if I can get a little rest. I need rest sadly."

" Yes, you look very tired," I said, in as ordinary a voice as I could manage, handing the keys back to him.

" Do I ? Well, to tell you the truth, I have been quite unable to sleep lately. I am so much disturbed by these hackney carmen who make it a practice to drive past the house at all hours of the night ; I hope they do not annoy you ? I have told them several times to go away, but they simply laugh at me. And the strange thing is," he continued, leaning over the rail of the corridor, and looking suspiciously down into the hall, " that though I gave orders that the lodge gates should always be locked at night, it does not stop them in the least—they just drive through them. Well, good-night, my dear," he said, nodding at me in a friendly way; "we must give it up for to-night, but we shall unearth Master Willy to-morrow."

He nodded again, and walked away down the corridor.

CHAPTER XXVII.

THAT night the wind shifted to the south-west, and the storm that came thundering in from the Atlantic was the worst I had known since I came to Durrus. The rain had been coming down in furious floods ever since sunset, and as the night darkened in, the wind dashed it against my window till I thought the sashes must give way. The roaring of the storm in the trees never ceased, and once or twice, through the straining and lashing of the branches, I heard the crash of a falling bough. The house was full of sounds : the rattling of the ill-fitting windows, the knocking of the picture-frames against the walls of the corridor, the loud drip of water from a leak in the skylight. Somewhere in the house a door was banging incessantly. It maddened me to hear it, more especially now, when I was trying to determine by the sound if the door which had just been opened was that of Uncle Dominick's room. His door had been open, and his room dark, when I had passed it on my way up to bed an hour ago.

The next day was Tuesday. The storm raged steadily on, putting out of the question all possibility

of going out. The shutters on the western side of
the house were all closed, and I sat in the semi-
darkness of the library, trying to read, and looking
from time to time through the one unshuttered
window out on to the gravel sweep. Broken twigs
and pieces torn from the weather-slated walls were
strewed over the ground. A great sycamore had
fallen across the drive a little below the house, and
the other trees swung and writhed as if in despair
at the long stress of the gale.

Roche came in and out of the room on twenty
different pretexts during the day, and made each an
occasion for ventilating some new theory to explain
Willy's absence. I was kneeling on the window-
seat, looking out into the turmoil, as the wind hurried
the black rain-clouds across the sky, and the gloomy
daylight faded into night, when he came into the
room again.

" There's a great dhraught from that window,
miss," he remarked. " You'd be best let me shut
the shutthers. You'll see no sign of Masther Willy
this day, unless he's coming by the last thrain.
The masther's asking for him the whole day. He's
very unaisy in his mind. He's roaming, roaming
through the house all the day, and he's give ordhers
to have his dinner sent to his own room. He wasn't
best pleased when he found Masther Willy had locked
up the room that's next your own, and twice, an' I
coming upstairs, I seen him sthriving to open the
door."

" Master Willy did that to prevent Moll getting

in there," I explained. " I will tell the master so myself."

" Don't say a word to him, miss, good nor bad," said Roche, shaking his knotted forefinger at me expressively. " He'll forget—he'll forget——" He sniffed significantly, and, as if to prevent himself from saying any more, he shuffled out of the room.

But Willy did not come by the last train ; indeed, the storm was still too violent for any one to travel. I lay awake the greater part of the night, filled with feverish fears and fancies. Several times I could have been sure that I heard some one wandering about the house, and once I thought there was a shaking and pushing at the locked door of the room next to mine.

When I awoke next morning, I found that the wind had been at length beaten down by a deluge of rain, which was descending in a grey continuous flood, as if it never meant to stop. The day dragged wearily on. Roche had spoken truly in saying that Uncle Dominick was uneasy and restless. It seemed to me that he never stopped walking about the house. I heard him constantly moving backwards and forwards, from the library to his own study ; and once the sound of footsteps in Willy's room overhead startled me for an instant into wondering if Willy had come home.

The long waiting and suspense had got on my nerves, and the gloom and silence made the house seem like a prison. I could neither read nor play the piano. I was debarred from even the society of Pat and Jinny, as, on the first day of the storm, their muddy footmarks in the hall had made my uncle angrily order their exile to the stable. By luncheon-time the rain had nearly spent itself. The wind went round into the north-west, and a wet gleam of sunshine suddenly shone out on the trees, making every branch and twig show with pale distinctness against the bank of purple cloud behind. A pilot-boat was beating into Durrusmore Harbour in the teeth of the cold wind ; the curlews screamed fitfully as they flew inland. It was not a pleasant afternoon, but I was thankful for the chance of getting out of the house.

The shrubberies were chilly and dripping, and their walks were covered with soaking withered leaves, but they were sheltered from the wind. I had come to the place where I had once left the path to gather ferns by the stream, when, at the angle where the two paths meet, I came suddenly upon Willy.

He was sitting on a tumble-down old rustic seat, with his elbows on his knees, and his face hidden in his hands.

" Willy ! " I cried, starting forward, " where have you been ? what is the matter ? Are you ill ? "

He raised his head, and looked at me vacantly, and for the moment I felt almost as great a shock as if I had seen him lying dead there ; if he had been dead, his whole look could hardly be more changed than it was now. A bluish-grey pallor had taken the place of his usually fresh colouring ; his eyes were sunk in dark hollows, but the lids were red ; and I saw, with shame at surprising them there, the traces of tears on his cheeks.

"I'm all right," he answered, turning his face away without getting up; "please don't stay here, Theo. It's only that my head's pretty bad."

A discoloured sheet of blue foolscap paper was lying on the seat beside him, and he put it into the pocket of his coat while he was speaking. I was too bewildered to move.

"You'd better go in," he said again; "it's awfully cold and wet for you to be out here."

The feeling that I was prying upon his trouble, whatever it was, made me take a few undecided steps away from him; but, looking back, I saw that he had again relapsed into his old position, and with an uncontrollable impulse I came back.

"I won't go away, Willy," I said, sitting down beside him; "I can't leave you here like this. Won't you tell me what has happened? What has kept you away? We've been awfully anxious about you!"

He neither lifted his head nor spoke, but I could hear the quick catchings of his breath. A thrust of sharp pity pierced my heart.

"Do tell me what it is, Willy," I repeated, careless of the break in my voice, putting one hand on his shoulder, and trying with the other to draw one of his from his face.

He was trembling all over, and when I touched him he started and let his hand fall, but he turned still further from me.

"Don't," he said huskily. "You can't do **any** good ; nothing can——"

"What do you mean ? " I said, horror-struck at the settled despair in his voice. "What has happened to you ? "

"It's no use your asking me questions," he answered more calmly. "I tell you there's nothing the matter with me."

"I don't believe you," I said. "Something *has* happened to you since I saw you. Is it anything that I have done ? Is it my fault in any way ? "

"No, it is not your fault." He stood up, and went on wildly, without looking at me, "But I wish I had died before you came to Durrus ! I wish I was in the graveyard out there this minute ! I wish the whole scheming, infernal crew were in hell—I wish——"

"Oh, stop, Willy ! " I cried—" stop ! You are frightening me ! "

He had been standing quite still, but he had flung out his clenched hand at every sentence, and his grey eyes were fixed and dilated.

"I don't know what I'm saying ; I didn't mean to frighten you," he said, sitting down again beside me. "I had no right to say that—about wishing I was dead before you came. Your coming here was the best thing ever happened to me in my life. I'll always thank God for giving me the chance of loving you ; and no matter what happens, I always will love you—always—always——"

He caught my hand as if he were going to draw me towards him, but, checking himself, he let it fall with a groan.

"It's all over now," he said. "Everything's gone to smash."

A rush of wind shivered through the laurels, and shook a quick rattle of drops from the shining leaves.

"Why should it all be over? Why should not it begin again?"

I said it firmly, but it seemed to me as if I were listening to some one else speaking.

"What do you mean?" He stared at me.

"I mean that perhaps I made a mistake," I said, beginning to hesitate—"that perhaps, that night at Mount Prospect, I was wrong in what I said to you——"

"You're humbugging me!" he said fiercely, without taking his eyes from my face. "You don't know what you're saying."

"Yes, I do know," I answered, still with that feeling that another person was speaking for me. "I've thought about it before now, and I thought perhaps if you would forgive——"

"Forgive! I don't understand you. Do you mean to say you would marry me?"

"Yes."

He looked at me stupidly, and staggered to his feet as if he were drunk.

"I'm having a fine time of it!" he said, with a loud harsh laugh. "She says she'll have me after all, and I've got to say ' No, thank you ! ' "

He swayed as he stood opposite to me, and then, falling on his knees, he laid his head on my lap, and broke into desperate sobbing.

CHAPTER XXVIII.

I FOUND my uncle standing in the hall when I came downstairs to dinner.

" What a terrible day this has been ! " he said, as he offered me his arm. " This rain makes the air so oppressive," he sighed, " and I have much to trouble me."

He helped me to soup, and having done so, got up and walked over to the fireplace. " I have no appetite at all," he said, " I suppose it is caused by want of sleep, but I really have a positive horror of food."

He turned his back to me and leaned his forehead against the high mantel-shelf, while I went on with dinner as well as I could.

Since Willy had left me, left me sitting stupefied on the shrubbery seat, with the rain beating down through the laurels upon me, I had not seen or heard anything of him. He had gone without another word of explanation ; all was dark and threatening, and my heart was heavy with apprehension.

I think I never was as fond of Willy, or as truly unhappy about him as now, just after I had, incredibly, asked him to marry me, and had, inexplicably, been rejected. My own point of view was

9

forgotten in the consuming desire to understand the mystery. There was no adequate solution, but the gusty booming of the wind in the chimney, and the drumming of the many-fingered rain against the window, brought home the one tangible fact that Willy was still out of the house on one of the worst nights of the year.

Uncle Dominick raised his head as if listening, and came back to the table.

" I am forgetful of my duties," he said, speaking very carefully, and as if he were saying a lesson, " will you not take a glass of wine ? you must be tired after your long drive in the snow from Carrickbeg."

I stared. " But I have not been out driving to-day."

He put his hand to his head. " How forgetful I am ! " he said hastily, " but the fact is I am so upset by anxiety about Willy that I scarcely know what I am saying. I confused Carrickbeg with Esker—till a few years ago Carrickbeg was our nearest station, and in those days travellers did not arrive here till one o'clock in the morning—one o'clock on a cold snowy morning," he slowly repeated to himself with a shudder. He poured himself out a glass of port, and, having drunk it, again left his chair and stood by the fire, fidgeting with a trembling hand with the objects on the mantel-shelf. Dinner was soon over, and, not liking to leave Uncle Dominick, I drew a chair over to the fire and sat down. He did not seem to notice me, but began to pace up and down the room, stopping now and then by one of the windows as if listening for sounds outside ; but the noisy splashing of the water that fell from a broken eaveshoot on to the gravel, was all that was to be heard.

"There ! " he said at last, in a whisper ; " do you hear the footsteps ? Do you hear them coming ? "

I jumped up and listened too. "No, I can hear nothing."

"I *did* hear them," he said positively. "I know they are beginning."

I could not understand what he meant, but I went to the nearest window, and was beginning to unbar the shutters, when there came a loud ring at the hall-door bell.

"I told you he was coming," my uncle said. "I must get out some brandy for him after his long drive in the snow."

The hall door was opened, and I heard Roche's voice. I ran to the door, and, opening it, met Willy coming into the room.

His face was all wet with rain, and his hair was hanging in damp points on his forehead. He walked past me into the room. My uncle stood still by the window, holding with one hand to the heavy folds of the red curtain.

"What ! Willy ! " he said, coming forward, and staring at Willy with wild eyes in which frightened conjecture slowly steadied into reassurance. "Was it *you* who came to the door ? " A sort of sob shook his voice. "My dear boy, I am rejoiced to see you ; but, good heavens, how wet you are ! "—going to the sideboard and pouring out a glass of brandy. "Here, you must drink this at once."

"I don't want it," said Willy; "I don't want anything."

He stood still, looking at his father, who, from some cause or other, was shaking in every limb.

"Where have you been since I saw you, Willy?" I faltered.

"I don't know—walking about in the rain. I've got something to say to you," he went on, addressing his father. "You needn't go away, Theo; you might as well hear it too."

Uncle Dominick lifted the glass of brandy to his lips, and swallowed it at a gulp.

"Well, my dear boy," he said, with a smile, and in a stronger voice, "let us hear what you have got to say."

"It's easy told," Willy said, putting his hands into his pockets. "I was married to Anstey Brian at the priest's house this morning."

CHAPTER XXIX.

THERE was dead silence for some seconds. Uncle Dominick was the first to break it.

" You married her ? " he said slowly, the words falling from his lips like drops of acid. " You mean to say she is your wife ? "

Willy nodded stubbornly.

My uncle stood looking at him, the blood mounting in dark waves to his pale face, till I should scarcely have known him. He made a stammering attempt to speak, and moved some steps forward towards Willy, groping with his hands in front of him as if he were blind, before the words came.

" Leave the house ! " he gasped, in a high, shrill voice—" leave the house ! "—swaying as if shaken by the passion that filled him—" or I will kick you out like a dog ! "

He stopped again to take breath, but recovering himself caught at the collar of Willy's coat as if to put his threat into execution.

" You needn't trouble yourself," said Willy, raising his arm and retreating before his father's onslaught. " You've seen pretty nearly the last of me now ; but, whether you like it or no, I'm going to stay here for to-night."

Uncle Dominick grasped at the edge of the sideboard to steady himself, his face so dark and swollen that I thought he was going to have a fit.

"Stay here!" he roared. "Stay here! I'll see you damned before you spend another night in this house!"

"Now, look here," said Willy, in a hard, overbearing voice, keeping his eyes fixed on his father's face, "it'll be the best of your play to keep quiet. I'm going to stay here, and that's the end of it!"

His insolent manner appeared to cow my uncle. The colour began to fade from his face, and his expression became more controlled, though it was more evil than ever when he spoke next.

"And your bride? May I ask if she has done me the honour of coming here?" He wiped a thin foam from his lower lip with his trembling hand. "Or is she perhaps at her father's residence?"

Willy turned his face so that I could not see it. "She's gone to Cork," he said. "And I'm going to Australia with her to-morrow."

"I suppose you intend eventually to return here after your honeymoon?" my uncle went on, with a nasty smile, pouring out and drinking another glass of brandy, while he waited for Willy's reply.

"I've done with this place for ever," answered Willy steadily, looking straight at his father. "I married Anstey Brian for a reason that may-be you know as well as I do!"

"What do I know about your reasons for degrading yourself?" interrupted my uncle, dashing his hand down upon the sideboard with a return of his first fury. " I know the reason you'll be given credit for—and very rightly too, no doubt ! "

" I say once for all," said Willy, whiter than ever, but standing like a rock, " and I say it before God, that you or any one else who says that is a liar ! "

" Very heroic ! very chivalrous ! " said my uncle, with an attempt at chilly sarcasm that was belied by his panting breath. " That is of course as it may be, but I know at all events one thing about her, and that is, she shall get no good of her infamous plotting !——" the glasses on the sideboard clashed and rang as he struck it again. " You shall never own a stick or a stone of Durrus ! " he shrieked. " Your cousin shall have it all—your cousin shall get everything I have ! I will see to that this very night ! "

" Oh, all right," Willy answered coolly ; " the sooner the better. But I may as well tell you that if you went down on your knees to me this minute, I wouldn't touch a halfpenny, nor the value of one that belonged to you. I've money enough to take me to Australia, and when I go away to-morrow morning it will be for good and all."

I had up to this stood by a scared and silent spectator ; but now I tried to make my voice heard.

" I won't have it," I said, half choked with my own eagerness. " It is no use leaving it to me ; I won't have your money ! "

Uncle Dominick took no notice of me at all. He had sunk down on the chair nearest him, his passion having seemingly exhausted his strength, and his hand on the table beside him shook and twisted as if he had lost all control over its muscles.

Willy spoke to me for the first time.

" See here, Theo," he said gently, also ignoring my protest, " you'd better go on upstairs out of this; you can't do any good here." He glanced at his father. " Do go now, like a good girl; he and I have got things to settle before I go."

He put his hand on my shoulder, and half pushed me to the door.

" Promise you won't let him do that," I said, trying to hold the door as he opened it. " Tell him I won't have it."

He did not answer; but, disengaging my fingers from their grasp of the door, he held them in his for an instant.

" I'll see you again," he said; and then shut the door and left me standing outside.

I waited for a long time in the drawing-room, but Willy did not come. Ten and eleven struck; the fire died out, and the candles on the chimney-piece burned down till the paper which fitted them into their sockets took fire and began to flare smokily. I went out into the hall and listened, but could hear no sound of voices. Some one was moving about upstairs. Perhaps Willy had gone up by the back stairs from the dining-room. Perhaps he had changed his mind and did not want to see me after all, I thought, making my way up to my room in a stupor of fatigue and misery.

There was a light under his door when I passed,

and I stopped uncertainly outside. He was dragging boxes about, and opening and shutting drawers; evidently he was packing. Should I call him? This would be my last chance of seeing him, as he was going away by the early train in the morning. But with the thought, the remembrance of Anstey fell like a shadow between him and me. What could I say to him if I were to see him? How could I ignore the subject which must be uppermost in both our minds? And yet, how could I bring myself to speak of it? Most likely he had felt this same difficulty, and had purposely avoided meeting me.

I went slowly on from his door, and into my own room, trying to realise the impossible thought that I had seen the last of Willy. Willy, the trusty comrade of many a day's careless pleasuring; who had taken me out schooling and ferreting, and had ransacked every hedge to cut for me superfluous members of the flattest of blackthorns, and the straightest of ash plants—Willy, with whom I used to gossip and wrangle and chaff in the easiest of intimacy; who had been, as he himself would have expressed it, the "best play-boy" I had ever known. Willy married to Anstey Brian, and going away for ever to-morrow morning, and going without even saying good-bye!—these were things too hard and too sorry to be taken in easily.

A knock came at my door.

"Theo, are you there? Could I see you for a minute?"

I opened the door and went out into the corridor.
Willy was standing there in his shirt-sleeves.

" I heard you coming up," he began quickly, " and
I came to say ' Good-bye.' "

" Oh, Willy ! " I said wretchedly, " are you really
going ? "

" Yes ; I'm off by the early train," he answered.
" It's late now ; I won't keep you up." He put out
his hand to me. " Good-bye," he said.

I took his hand, and held it, unable to say a word.

" Good-bye," he repeated, in a whisper.

" Willy," I cried suddenly, " why did you do it ?
Why did you do it ? "

" I can't tell you—I had to. May-be, some
day——" he broke off. " One thing I can tell
you, anyhow, is that this place belongs to you,
or ought to. I was shown a will two days ago
by—by those who had stolen it—or what I con-
sider as good as a will, and I was told more
besides—Please God you, nor no one'll ever know !
It's all right now, anyhow, I've stopped their
mouths, and the Governor's left the place to you.
He did it this very night."

" Never ! Never ! " I said, scarcely able to get
the words out, but possessed by one unshakable
determination. " I don't care what has happened or
what any one may have done. I will never have
it ! "

" You don't know what you're saying," he
said with a strange gentleness ; " if you've any
regard for me you'll say no more now. I've had

about as much as I can stand." Then with an effort : " I must go. Will you say 'Good-bye' to me ? "

" I will," I said, carried away by the restrained misery of his voice, and putting my arms round his neck. " You've been too good to me—oh, Willy, my dear, I've brought you nothing but bad luck. Good-bye."

I kissed his cheek—he was my only cousin, and I was never going to see him again—and then I tried to draw myself away from the grasp that was tightening round me, but it was too late.

" I'll never say 'Good-bye' to you," he said fiercely, straining me to him. " I won't let you go till you tell me if you meant what you said to me in the wood. Was it me you cared for, after all ? "

" Don't ask me," I implored. " Let me go ! "

" I won't ! " he answered, recklessly, trying to press his lips against mine.

I put my hands over my face, with a shrinking which told me in a moment the depth of the self-delusion which had carried me to the point of saying I would marry him. He must be told the truth now, no matter what it cost.

" I meant that I was fond of you," I said ; " but I never was in love with you."

" I see," he said bitterly. He let me go at once. " Then it was Nugent, after all."

I turned away without answering. At my own door I stopped, and again held out my hand.

"Willy," I said, breaking into tears, "say ' Good-bye.' "

He snatched my hand again, and kissed it many times ; he was crying too.

"God help us both ! " he said.   "Good-bye."

CHAPTER XXX.

In the thick dark of the January morning I heard Willy go.

Doors opened and shut; gleams of candle-light went past my bedroom door; luggage bumped down the stairs. The house was alive with footsteps and low voices. At last, and still in thick darkness, the grinding of the wheels on the gravel, Blackthorn's methodical, unconcerned trot dying away on the avenue, and, in the silence, the heart-shaking sobs of an old man—the sobbing of Roche in the hall as he shut the door upon the son of the house.

The day came at last, the implacable day, that must be lived and dealt with. I crept downstairs, feeling twenty years older, and on the hall table saw an unfamiliar hat and umbrella. The dining-room door opened and Roche met me.

"It wasn't eight o'clock this morning when I had to send for the docthor," he whispered hoarsely. "The masther's very bad. Yourself had better see the docthor; he's inside, ateing his breakfast now."

"What was the matter with the master?" I said, prepared now for any calamity that might befall.

Roche looked at me strangely. His collar was crumpled and his coat was torn.

"He was near killing the pair of us!" he whispered. "The docthor can tell ye!"

Little Doctor Kelly's vulgar, authoritative voice was quieter than I had ever known it, and his hot-tempered, light blue eye had in it the deference of sympathy.

"Sit down now," he said. "I asked Roche to send you here. I'm sorry to have to trouble you, but under the circumstances——" he hesitated, "it's an unfortunate business altogether——"

I silently awaited his tidings.

"Your uncle's in a very bad way," he said. "I've wired for a nurse—a man to look after him. He mustn't be left alone."

"What's the matter with him?" I said dully. "Is he dying?"

"I think not," said Doctor Kelly slowly. He looked hard at me. "I'm afraid, Miss Sarsfield, I must tell you that your uncle has been for years in the habit of drinking pretty hard, more than any one suspected, and this trouble about his son seems to have brought matters to a climax."

I had thought myself hardened against bad news, but I had not looked for anything so ugly, incongruous, degrading.

"Ought I to stay with him?" I said faintly. "I had made up my mind to go away this week, but I couldn't leave him like this."

"If you don't mind me telling you so," said Doctor

Kelly, " it would be the best thing you could do. You're not fit for a business of this kind. I understand all about the state of the case, and you're better out of it. Your uncle must be got into a private hospital, for the present at all events." He paused and rubbed his truculent red moustache. " Terrible affair this is about young Mr. Sarsfield," he went on. " Those people were too clever for him, and indeed I'm sorry for it. A fine young fellow if he'd been properly handled ! "

My averted and quivering face must have told its story ; he went abruptly back to the subject of my uncle.

" I'll go on and see The O'Neill now, and I'll speak to him about getting Mr. Sarsfield moved. I know he and his son have come back about a case he has in the Land Court. After all, he's his oldest friend here, and he's more fit to deal with the matter than you are. I wouldn't go near Mr. Sarsfield at all if I were you. He's quiet now, but you never can tell. Do nothing at all until O'Neill sees him."

Roche was waiting in the hall, and I heard Doctor Kelly's last words to him.

" Mind now there's somebody with him always. I'll send over the medicine."

I got through some breakfast, and went up to my room with the intention of getting out my trunks and doing some preliminary packing. They had been taken into the empty room next mine, the room that had been my father's, and that had, for her own inscrutable reasons, been haunted by Moll Hourihane.

I fetched the key and went into it to look for them. It felt cold, yet oppressively close; I opened the window and looked out into the mild still air. The sky was dark and sullen, with layers of overlapping clouds roofing it down to the horizon, and on the lonely sea stretches there was not so much as a fishing boat to be seen. I looked out at the woods of Durrus, motionless, bare, and wrapped in a quiet that it seemed nothing could break. By this time next week Willy and I would both be on the sea, speeding to opposite ends of the earth; it was I who had driven him from his home, and I abhorred the inheritance that he wished to thrust upon me. The tears crept to my eyes, and I turned from the window.

A book was lying on the floor, open at the title-page, and my father's name, in his own handwriting, caught my eye. I took it up and found that it was an old-fashioned pocket-book diary, shabby and battered, with dog's-eared leaves. It was dated the year of his death and there were entries in his writing on the first eleven days of the year, but the rest of the book was blank, save for the defilement of dirty finger-marks and the name " Mary Hourihane " written in pencil over and over again in an almost illegible scrawl. Here was Moll's handiwork again ; she had haunted what had been my father's room, and had mauled and defaced a relic that would have been priceless to my mother.

I sat down by the window and began to read the diary. Ten of the entries were merely brief records of the weather on his voyage from America, but on the 11th of January was written :—

" Arrived in Cork. Weather very cold. Wrote to Helen. Have caught severe cold but hope to get on to Durrus by to-morrow night. Am beginning to feel nervous as to my reception by my father and Dominick."

" *January* 12. Did not feel up to leaving by early train. Travelled on by later. Very cold, roads deep in snow. Had difficulty in hiring a car ; did not get to Durrus till 1 A.M. and then found that my impulse of reconciliation had come to me too late. My father died two days ago and was buried this afternoon."

The diary's record ceased.

" January 12th ! " I repeated to myself in bewilderment, " but my father died on the 9th, and he died in Cork ! " So my mother had told me, so the brass in Rathbarry Church set forth, stamping it into my memory during many Sunday mornings. My tired head struggled with the conflicting dates, and strained to recover possession of what it was that my mother had once said to me about the strange chance by which my father had missed inheriting the property. She had said that it was an unjust will, and an insulting one ; more I could not remember. I turned to the diary again, and re-read the meagre sentences. Then I noticed that there was a pocket in the cover with something in it. It was an envelope, addressed to my mother, with unused stamps on it ; it had been torn open, and there was only one sheet of note-paper in it. The ink had faded and the writing was weak.

" DURRUS, 13th *January*, 18—.

" DEAREST,

" I am at Durrus as you see. Would to God I had come here last year as you wished. My poor old father died the day before I landed at Queenstown, and my hope of being reconciled to him is now for ever at an end. I fear that my arrival was not only unexpected but undesired. Dominick received me very coldly, which was the more distressing as I felt, and still feel very unwell. I have not been out of bed since my arrival ; I fear I have a touch of pleurisy, brought on by a terrible cold drive here through snow in the middle of the night. Don't be frightened, it is not serious.

" The house is strangely deserted, and the only servant in it is that woman, Moll Hourihane, of whom I think I have spoken to you. She has always asserted herself to be the daughter of my Uncle Dick, and my father, whether rightly or no, has believed her to have a claim on the family, and has let her live in the house as a sort of housekeeper, a mistaken kindness, as I have always held. She has always been devoted to D. and my father, but has never liked me, nor I her, and as an attendant I find her neglectful and dirty. I asked D. for my friend Pat Roche, who was pantry-boy here when I was a child, and he said he had got so drunk at my father's funeral he had to send him home. I haven't seen little Willy. He was sent to the O'Neills when my father was taken

ill. You must begin to think of coming to me with the baby. Of course the place is mine now. D. has showed me the will. My father left the property to me, but expressly said that if I died before he did it was to go to Dominick. However there is no question of that now, and I will draft a will at once, and as soon as I can I shall have everything settled properly. I can hardly realise that in a month's time you and I may be together in the old home! Moll is waiting to post this for me, and indeed I do not feel up to writing more to-day. Good-bye, my dearest. I wish you were with me now. Your loving husband,

"OWEN."

Hot anger and impotent compassion at first drove out every other feeling. My father had lain helpless in this very room, victim of lies, of neglect, and low conspiracy. What loneliness, what longing for a tender and familiar hand had been his on his uncared-for death-bed, while his only brother and the hateful woman who had been his confederate looked on without pity. I sat down by the window and covered my face with my hands, afraid of these dark places of guilt in which I found myself. Was this what Willy had meant? Was this the secret for which he had sacrificed himself?

A stealing foot on the gravel outside made me start up again. I leaned out of the window, and saw Moll Hourihane approaching the French window of my uncle's study with stealthy swiftness. I had just time to notice that one of the doors was open, when Roche rushed out of it, and ran full against Moll, whose foot was already on the step. Something fell from under her shawl and crashed on the stone ; a tall brandy bottle, and the liquor splashed on the steps and over her bare feet. Roche flung her to one side.

" The masther ! " he shouted. " He's gone ! He's gone ! "

CHAPTER XXXI.

I was downstairs and out of the hall door in a moment.

I heard Roche's voice in the yard calling for help, and I ran to him. Already it seemed as if every soul in the establishment had congregated there, and Roche was loudly explaining what had happened.

" He was asleep, an' I slipped out to fill the hot bottle for his feet, an' when I come back he was gone, and the window open. I wasn't five minutes away from him. Run every side now, the whole o' ye! My God! don't stop lookin' at me! Let ye run. Ye wouldn't know what would he do!"

I turned and made for the back avenue, a quiet and shaded way, by which my uncle used to walk to the farm. I panted along it, and at every step my own inadequacy to cope with this horror daunted me, and the loss of Willy cut me to the heart. The anger had died in me; I saw only the wretched and distraught old man, driven by the devil that possessed him, wandering in a humiliation of grey hairs that was unbearable to think of.

There was no sign of him in or about the back avenue; I turned back and saw that Roche was

He looked shrewdly up at the branches over his head.

" I find it snug enough here, my dear," he said. His eyes met mine for the first time, and their shifty remoteness changed to a concentrated stare.

" Owen ! " he said, stepping backwards, and grop-ing with a tremulous hand for the tree behind him, " how did you get here ? You're dead !—I know you're dead ! You were dead when she brought me into the room "—he began to talk so fast that I could scarcely catch the words—" and then down at the edge of the pier, when she was tying the four-stone weight round your neck, I asked her if she was sure about it ; she said you were, and that you'd not come out of it till Poul-na-coppal ran dry. Is it dry ? " he screamed, " is it dry ? No one ever saw it dry ! Is this the end of the world——"

He collapsed on to his knees, and the book fell on the grass beside him.

" Almighty God ! " he babbled deliriously, " who has caused all Holy Scripture to be written for our learning——No ! that comes before the sermon——"

I heard the brushing and tramping of some one near us in the wood. My uncle's head was bent, he was muttering rapidly in some dark labyrinth of con-fusion and distress. He had forgotten me ; I crept in the direction of the footsteps. The first turn of the path took me out of sight of my uncle ; I began to run, calling in a low voice for Roche.

He answered with a shout, fifty yards away in the

tangled scrub, and before I could reach him he had called out :—

"Did ye see him? Where is he?"

When we reached the glade with the pine trees Uncle Dominick was gone. There was nothing there except the book, that sprawled face downwards on the grass.

CHAPTER XXXII

Soon afterwards I found myself standing at the edge of the wood, by a gateway that opened on to the bog. The gate had been flung wide open, and the wood was full of searchers. It was impossible that this could go on much longer. I leaned against the gate-post, and knew that I had come to the end of my strength.

Since yesterday afternoon blow upon blow had been dealt me, and the stupor of accumulated fatigue had fallen upon me. There was a weight in the air, the sky was low and foreboding, and a watery streak of yellow lay along the horizon behind the bog. A rook rustled close over my head with a subdued croak; I dully watched him flying quietly home to the tall elms by the lodge; he was still circling round them before settling down, when a long, wavering cry struck upon my ear, a sound that once heard is never forgotten, the cry of a woman keening. It came from the bog; every pulse stood still as I heard it, and I clung to the gate for support, while the varying ominous cadences filled the air. I knew, above and beyond reasoning, that it meant the end.

Already a messenger was running towards me along the bog track, shouting for help as he came.

" He's drowned ! He's drowned ! He's into Poul-na-coppal ! "

It was one of the stablemen, hatless, splashed with black mud.

" I was in the far wood," he gasped, " an' I seen him come to the edge of Poul-na-coppal, and Moll Hourihane follying him, an' when he seen her he jumped in ! There's no sign of him—I put a branch down in it—He's gone ! My God Almighty ! Do you hear her keening him now ! Her that never let a sound for twenty years ! "

Half a dozen men were now out of the wood, running across the bog, others pressed past me in the gateway. Roche caught me by the arm and thrust me back.

" Don't come in it, asthore ! " he said, the tears pouring down his ghastly face, " it's no good for ye."

Suddenly they were all gone ; I was alone, sitting on the edge of the path in the wood. One or two people ran past me, and I tried to follow them, but my knees failed me, and I sank down again, shivering and sick. I do not remember realising anything very clearly, except that I had reached the end of everything, and that there was no future. All that remained for me was to drag myself back to the desolate house on which I had brought ruin ; I lay prone on the dead leaves with my face on my arms, and the dry sobs tore at my chest.

" All right, that will do," said an authoritative voice at the gateway, " I can find her now."

I sat up, snatched again into the present by the ineradicable instinct that prompts us to hide our pain, startled into composure by the recognition of the voice.

"They told me you were here," said Nugent, standing in front of me, and speaking in a low and much moved voice. "I want you to come away from this—you mustn't stay here."

"I was going back to the house," I said, struggling to steady myself. "I shall be all right in a moment."

I tried to stand up, but almost failed ; he caught my hand and helped me. He did not release it, and that clasp became suddenly a living thing, telling what the pent heart could not utter. We stood, without a word to say, and convention fell from between us in the intense meaning of that silence. I had to raise my eyes to his ; they met, and there could no longer be any doubt. In spite of what seemed impossibility, in spite of all that fate had done or could do, we knew that we loved each other.

The drawing together, the meeting of the lips, the outrush of soul came without a word, irresistible and unexplainable ; the deepest, the dearest moment of life was ours, with calamity hemming it in, and powerless to touch it.

"Why did you send me away ? " he whispered.

"I never sent you away," I answered, bewildered.

"I was told that you were going to marry Willy."

"Who told you ? "

He hesitated. "It wasn't Willy," he said at last. "It doesn't matter now. Nothing matters now."

The means by which tenderness and healing can flow from heart to heart can never be tracked ; by some unknown sense they steal to us, beyond all power of expression, beyond what kisses can say.

" I believe you cared a great deal more for Willy than you did for me," Nugent said to me one evening when the hawthorn was in blossom, and the Clashmore woods were green.

" I don't know why I didn't," I answered, " but somehow, I always liked you best."

THE END.

PRINTED IN GREAT BRITAIN.
IMPRIMERIE NELSON, ÉDIMBOURG, ÉCOSSE.

THE EDINBURGH LIBRARY.

Cloth, 2s. net.

CHARLES DE BOURBON, CONSTABLE OF FRANCE.
Christopher Hare

ROBERT HERRICK. F. W. Moorman

MADAME DE BRINVILLIERS AND HER TIMES, 1630–1676. Hugh Stokes.

THE NEW JERUSALEM. G. K. Chesterton.

CONTEMPORARY PORTRAITS. Sir Algernon West.

TWO DIANAS IN ALASKA.
Agnes Herbert and a Shikári.

WILD LIFE IN A SOUTHERN COUNTY.
Richard Jefferies.

THE FOUR MEN. Hilaire Belloc.

SAMUEL PEPYS. Percy Lubbock.

JESUS, THE CARPENTER OF NAZARETH.
Robert Bird.

THE KINDRED OF THE WILD. C. G. D. Roberts

THE GREAT BOER WAR. A. Conan Doyle.

LIFE OF GLADSTONE. Herbert W. Paul.

THE FOREST. Stewart White.

THE GOLDEN AGE. Kenneth Grahame.

SIR HENRY HAWKINS.

FROM THE CAPE TO CAIRO. E. S. Grogan.

[Continued.

Cloth, 2s. net.

COLLECTIONS AND RECOLLECTIONS—II.
G. W. E. Russell.

A MODERN UTOPIA. H. G. Wells.

THE UNVEILING OF LHASA. E. Candler.

DREAM DAYS. Kenneth Grahame.

THE PATH TO ROME. Hilaire Belloc.

REMINISCENCES OF LADY DOROTHY NEVILL.

COLLECTED POEMS OF HENRY NEWBOLT.

POT-POURRI FROM A SURREY GARDEN. Mrs. Earle.

THE RING AND THE BOOK. Robert Browning.

THE ALPS FROM END TO END. Sir W. M. Conway.

A BOOK ABOUT ROSES. Dean Hole.

MEXICO AS I SAW IT. Mrs. Alec Tweedie.

FIELDS, FACTORIES, AND WORKSHOPS.
Prince Kropotkin.

CRUISE OF THE " FALCON." E. F. Knight.

THE PEOPLE OF THE ABYSS. Jack London.

NAPOLEON—THE LAST PHASE. Lord Rosebery.

SELF-SELECTED ESSAYS. Augustine Birrell.

FIJI TO THE CANNIBAL ISLANDS. B. Grimshaw.

FROM A COLLEGE WINDOW. A. C. Benson.

THE LAND OF FOOTPRINTS. Stewart White.

THE DESERT GATEWAY. S. H. Leeder.

[*Continued.*

EDINBURGH LIBRARY—*Contd.*

Cloth, 2s. net.

MARSHAL MURAT. Capt. A. H. Atteridge.

MY FATHER. Estelle W. Stead.

WITH THE RUSSIAN PILGRIMS TO JERUSALEM.
Stephen Graham.

A WOMAN IN THE BALKANS. Mrs. Gordon.

ITALIAN CHARACTERS. Countess Cesaresco.

THROUGH THE MAGIC DOOR. A. Conan Doyle.

HUNTING CAMPS IN WOOD AND WILDERNESS.
H. Hesketh Prichard.

ABRAHAM LINCOLN. Brand Whitlock.

THE HAUNTERS OF THE SILENCES. C. G. D. Roberts.

WITH POOR EMIGRANTS TO AMERICA. S. Graham.

WATCHERS OF THE TRAILS. C. G. D. Roberts.

IN THE COUNTRY OF JESUS. Mathilde Serao.

RECREATIONS OF AN HISTORIAN. G. Trevelyan.

GARIBALDI'S DEFENCE OF THE ROMAN REPUBLIC.
G. Trevelyan.

GARIBALDI AND THE MAKING OF ITALY.
G. Trevelyan.

GARIBALDI AND THE THOUSAND. G. Trevelyan.

FABRE'S BOOK OF INSECTS.

THE BOOK OF A NATURALIST. W. H. Hudson.

JOHN BUNYAN. By the Author of "Mark Rutherford."

T. Nelson & Sons, Ltd., London, Edinburgh, and New York.